BLACK
HEART

Note from the Author

This is a first edition of my first book.

There are a few mistakes in here that got past the proof-reading.

The book has since been re-edited and re-issued.

Hope you enjoy this version and please leave a review on Amazon.

Cheers

BLACK
HEART

JEFFREY J. GOULD

authorHOUSE®

AuthorHouse™
1663 Liberty Drive
Bloomington, IN 47403
www.authorhouse.com
Phone: 1-800-839-8640

© *2012 by Jeffrey J. Gould. All rights reserved.*

No part of this book may be reproduced, stored in a retrieval system, or transmitted by any means without the written permission of the author.

Published by AuthorHouse   10/27/2012

ISBN: 978-1-4772-3855-4 (sc)
ISBN: 978-1-4772-3856-1 (hc)
ISBN: 978-1-4772-3857-8 (e)

Any people depicted in stock imagery provided by Thinkstock are models, and such images are being used for illustrative purposes only.
Certain stock imagery © Thinkstock.

This book is printed on acid-free paper.

Because of the dynamic nature of the Internet, any web addresses or links contained in this book may have changed since publication and may no longer be valid. The views expressed in this work are solely those of the author and do not necessarily reflect the views of the publisher, and the publisher hereby disclaims any responsibility for them.

About the author

Jeff Gould was born in the north east of England in 1960. He grew up in Nottingham.

In 1980 he joined The Royal Air Force and served in The Falklands, Cyprus, Germany and UK. bases, including RAF Lyneham and Brize Norton.

Always keen on birds of prey, upon leaving the military, he became a professional falconer.

Through falconry he travelled extensively throughout South Africa, working for a non-profit organisation dedicated to the conservation of birds of prey and other wildlife.

Jeff now lives in Norfolk, East Anglia, with his wife and family.

I would like to thank the following people
Jenny, Kerry and Russ.Tony Smith,Liam Harvey and finally Jonty and my other mates at the Banham Barrel.

I'd like to dedicate this book to my kids (in alphabetical order to avoid grief!)

Amy, Chris, Ellie, Joanne and Matthew.

Chapter one

Thursday 23 February 2012

The first was my wife. Bitch.

She hadn't been expecting me home for another day or so. She wasn't exactly the faithful sort. That wasn't entirely her fault. She was a very attractive woman, not exactly short of admirers, and I was often away from home. Sometimes she knew where. Sometimes she even knew roughly when I was due back. Not often though.

We didn't have any kids. We'd had the tests. She was infertile. Just as well really, or God knows how many other mens kids would be running around calling me daddy?

I'd managed to cadge a lift on a USAF C130 out of Kabul en route to RAF Mildenhall in Suffolk. I could've booked into the mess, but instead hired a car and drove home. I thought about ringing ahead to say that I was on my way. Instead I decided to surprise her.

I did that alright!

As I pulled into our close I noticed a black BMW in our driveway. I drove past and parked at the side of the road. As I walked up the drive to the house I noticed a 'For Sale' sign in the back window of the 'Beamer.'

Black Heart

There were no lights on in the house except for the bedroom. I turned my key in the front door. The noises eminating from our bedroom were difficult not to hear as I stood at the foot of the stairs. It was pretty obvious to me that our mystery guest hadn't popped round for a game of chess.
Fighting my first instinct, which was to tear up the stairs and kick the shit out of both of them, instead I went back outside, closing the door silently behind me.
I stood in the shadows at the side of the house and lit a cigarette.
'Think Charlie, like you've been trained to do' I told myself.
By the time I'd finished my cig I had a plan.
I memorised the registration number of the BMW. I also memorised the cell-phone number on the 'For Sale' sign. As I passed the car I smashed one of the rear lights with my heel. Using my cell-phone as a torch I picked up the broken pieces of red plastic and put them in my pocket.
I returned to the hire car and drove to Wooton Bassett.
Just outside the town I pulled over at the side of the road. I took out my cell-phone and swapping my sim-card for a spare, I phoned the jerk. After several rings he answered.
He sounded a little out of breath. Wonder why? I knew my wife was close to him (possibly attached) so I spoke quietly, in an Irish accent. I asked him if he still had the car for sale and was he at

home as I would come round now. After a few embarrassed 'ums and ers' from him, I eventually arranged to meet him. I told him that I was going away for a few days on business but could meet him in Wooton Basset in 20minutes. If I liked the car I would give him a £500 deposit and pay the balance in a week. He took the bait.

I hung up and ditched the sim-card, along with the broken pieces of his tail-light down a nearby drain. I then drove back in the direction of my house. About a mile from home I passed the black BMW heading the other way. I pulled up just beyond my driveway.

As I walked towards the house I spotted a tie near where the Beamer had been parked. I picked it up and continued to the house. Inside, I walked silently up the stairs to our bedroom. The door was open. The bedclothes were in total disarray and there were empty take-away cartons littering the floor. On the bedside tables were empty wine bottles and glasses. Down the hall I heard the sound of the toilet flushing. I stood behind the bedroom door as I heard the sound of the bathroom light being swithed off and the door opening.

I wrapped the tie around my knuckles and as she entered the bedroom I pounced.

Black Heart

I had grabbed her from behind but could clearly see the look of surprise and horror on her face reflected in the dressing table mirror as the tie squeezed the life from her. I let her lifeless body slip to the floor. I dropped the tie next to her and went downstairs. I picked up the phone and dialled 999.

Chapter two

The Police actually arrived fairly quickly. A pair of traffic cops had been pretty close to my address when I'd dialled 999. One of them went upstairs to confirm my report that the wife was indeed dead. The second took out his notebook and began to take a statement from me. I told him that I'd arrived home to find a black BMW parked in my drive. As I'd parked up the 'beamer' had reversed out and taken off at speed in the direction of Wooton Bassett. I hadn't really noticed the driver, other than it was a white male. I did however notice that the car had a rear light out and that the registration number was something, something DMG. I also said that there was a 'For Sale' sign in the back and that the phone number ended in 7686. The cop got on his radio and passed the vehicle details to his dispatch.

Before long it was chaos. Ambulance, scenes-of-crime, marked and unmarked cop cars all converged on our previously quiet neighbourhood. The curtains up and down the close were certainly twitching.

As I sat on the doorstep smoking a cigarette I watched the cop who had taken my statement. He was busy bringing a plain-clothed 'Rupert' up to speed.

Black Heart

A few minutes later he approached me. He introduced himself to me as DI Jenkins and showed his ID, just in case I didn't believe him. He was a right smarmy 'graduate' type. It was obvious that to him I was the prime suspect.

Well I suppose I was the husband and I did discover the body. After confirming with me that I was the husband and that I had found the body DI 'Dickhead' proceeded, in a rather sarcastic tone, to praise me on my amazing powers of observation regarding the BMW. I told him that in my line of work, it payed to be observant. I showed him my ID and that changed his attitude! I could see he was lost for words. He was rescued from his embarrassment by one of his colleagues who had rushed over to tell him that the BMW had been located and that the driver had been arrested and was being taken to the station.

First 48. In the TV program its 48hrs. The 'Keystone Cops' here were solving crimes in 48 minutes!

Chapter three

I went back to the Police station with the two traffic cops. It was pretty busy back there, press, even a TV crew. I don't suppose they get too many murders in these parts. As we were entering the main doors a couple of marked cars and a white van pulled up outside. We stepped aside as a man in handcuffs, with a coat draped over his head, was lead through to the front desk. I watched as he was signed in and read his rights by the desk sergeant.
'David Michael Gross you are charged . . . .
What a cock I thought. DMG—David Michael Gross.
I was lead past him to an interview room to make a detailed statement. Half way through the process I was interrupted by the DI who came in to get my wifes next of kin details.Looked like he'd got the unpleasant job of informing them. Once I'd finished I popped outside for a ciggy. While I was out there I phoned my ops room. My CO phoned me back 10mins later with his condolences. He put me on compassionate leave. I went back inside to arrange some digs for the night. Well I couldn't go home could I?
My house was a murder scene.

I told the desk sergeant that I needed to get a room for the night. He passed me a local rag.

'There are a couple of pubs in the village sir. The Crown and The Lion. Nothing fancy, but they're ok.' He said, turning the phone so that I could use it.

As I stood flicking through the mag, out of the corner of my eye I saw the door to one of the interview rooms open. A uniformed cop came out of the room carrying a plastic bag containing Gross's clothes and presumably his shoes, as I could see him sitting at the desk, bare-foot, wearing a paper suit. He looked very confused and stressed. The door closed and the uniform brought the bag to the desk sergeant to get it logged as evidence.

I found an advertisement for the Crown and dialled the number. The girl who answered informed me that they were fully booked. They'd had a rush on the rooms but said I should try the Lion. She gave me the number. I wondered if the Lion would do the same for them. I didn't need to wait long for the answer to that question because when I rang the Lion I was informed by the guy who answered that they were full, but I could try the Crown. Fuck me. I was single-handedly boosting the local economy! Maybe I should run for mayor!

Chapter four

Eventually I managed to get a room in a small B&B on a farm, about a mile outside the village. I was told that it was too late for dinner. I told the woman that was ok I wasn't hungry. That was a lie for the desk sergeant's benefit-I was fucking starving! He was obviously listening as he then turned to the young PC, who looked about 12 (sign your getting old when cops look like kids, as my old man always says) and told him to give me a lift to the farm. I told him I'd rather have a lift to my house to get my hire car as it contained all of my luggage. 'You can't go there sir, it's a murder scene.' He then went bright red, realising that he'd been less than diplomatic by reminding me of my wife's demise. 'I don't see what the problem is sergeant my car isn't at the house. I didn't park in my drive on account of a fucking BMW being in my parking slot! Apart from anything else I need my kit. I'm minging, I've been travelling for over 24hrs' 'Better not sir . . .' Just then the DI came out of the interview room, looking very pleased with himself. 'Well?' I said. 'Far too early at this stage sir, but let's just say we aren't looking for anyone else in relation to this matter.'

Black Heart

'Matter?' I said in my best 'my wife's been murdered and you're calling it a matter' voice.

'Sorry sir, I didn't mean to be so . . . indelicate. The suspect has admitted that he was at your house. He admits that he . . . . well that he had sex with your wife, and has done so on several other occasions. However, he insists that your wife was alive and well when he left and has now clammed up and won't say another word until he's seen a brief.' 'So, what happens next?'

'We wait til his brief turns up and then we will continue questioning him.'

'Ok.' I said 'now have a word with your sergeant here, and tell him I need my car, or more to the point, my kit.'

'I don't see why not' he said, then to the sergeant.

'Get young Paul here to drop Mr Higgins off at his car. Do we have an address and contact number for him?'

The sergeant nodded. The DI turned to me 'We'll be in touch sir.' Passing me his card he continued. 'If there is anything else you think of, or any questions, don't hesitate to give me a call.'

Then to the sergeant 'Get that bloody kettle on Alf, it's going to be a long night.'

As we drove to my house to pick up my car, the young bobby was trying to be pleasant.

'The DI is a bit of a pompous arse, but he is very good at his job sir. That Gross is gonna get his!'

'Yes I'm sure he is' I agreed.

'I mean, we've got your eye-witness account of him leaving your house. He's admitted, well you know, being with your wife. His finger prints and DNA are going to be all over the place. Sorry sir, by the way I'm PC Paul. Paul Paul. Yes I know I get a lot of stick about it. But yea, the bit I don't get is why the arsehole stops off at the Lion for a pint? I mean why didn't he just keep going? Dozy git had parked on the road outside the pub. We'd got a good description of the vehicle, thanks to you. One of the cars responding to your address drove straight past it! PC Collins it was. He just called for back-up and waited for the joker to walk to his car. Bingo. You're knicked sonny!'

I think our Paul Paul watches too many episodes of 'The Sweeney.'

We pulled up opposite my house.

'Suppose we'll be seeing each other again soon.' Said Paul

'Yeah I suppose so. Thanks for the lift.'

As I walked to my hire car and opened it, I noticed my driveway was taped off with Police tape. Every light in the house was on and there were spotlights on the drive and in the garden.
I can't wait for my electricity bill. For fucks sake! I drove the few miles to my B&B.

Chapter five

I slowed down as I approached the sharp bend where I seemed to remember seeing the B&B sign. I'd lived around here for about 5 years now but knew very little about the area. I say 5 years. I'd probably spent 4 of those 5 years elsewhere. No wonder my wife was such a slapper. Whenever I'd been at home I'd tended to do most of my socialising, shopping etc in Swindon.

I pulled into the little track that led to the farmhouse where I would be staying. I checked in with the old dear, who showed me to my room and told me breakfast would be between 7.30 and 9.00. She told me all the rooms were full.

'Lucky I'm not charging you commission!' I thought to myself.

I had a quick shower. I needed one. Sitting on the bed in a towel I flicked through the local rag. That would do. The 'Happy Kebab.' It was on the High Street in Wooton Bassett, opposite the Lion public house. Kebab, couple of pints, then, a good kip.

Although the B&B was less than a couple of miles from Wooton Bassett, I decided to drive rather than walk. It was getting late and I was hungry.

At the kebab shop I ordered a large chicken donner with chips, salad and chilli sauce.

Black Heart

'Eat in or take out?' The guy asked me. I glanced around the small café. There were a few small tables in the window. Warmer than sitting in the car I decided.
'Eat in' I replied.
'10 minutes' he said. I paid him and stepped outside. Before I realised what I'd done, I'd sparked up my third fag of the day. The week, probably.
That's when I saw him.
Number two.
The fat bastard. I wouldn't have thought it possible, but he was even fatter than the last time I'd seen him. I'd sworn to myself that if I got the chance he would pay for what he'd done to my mate Jimmy. As I watched, he wobbled from the car park and across the road. Stepping up the kerb outside the Lion seemed a major struggle for him. He squeezed through the doors and into the pub. I'd thought about a beer or two after my kebab, seeing John Kenny wobble into the lion made a visit to the pub a definite.
As I sat at the table eating my scran, I thought back to the first time I encountered our Mr Kenny. It was about 5 years ago now, not long after I'd moved to the area. He was the landlord of the Lion. He wasn't a local. In fact he was a bit of a 'cockney wide-boy.' Wide in more ways than one!

He was also a bully. He thought of himself as a bit of a hard-man and in 'His Pub' he was an obnoxious git. I got off to a bad start with him. I'd called in at the Lion one evening, and was sat at the bar, sipping a pint and reading the pub newspaper. I use that term loosely, it was 'The Sun.' No shocks there, Kenny didn't strike me as a 'Telegraph' man.

Kenny, who had been busy acting 'hard' to a couple of youngsters, suddenly turned his attention to me.

'Oh. Oh stranger. Do you play pool?' Without waiting for a reply he slammed a 50 pence piece on the bar next to me.

'Rack em!' He said. Kenny also apparently rated himself as the best pool player in the area.On the planet probably. Well I'm not one to turn down a challenge. As it happens I'm not a bad player, though I say so myself.

'What rules do you play?' I asked as I put the coin in the slot and released the balls.

'New World' he said as he screwed together his two-piece cue with his podgy hands. As I placed the balls in the triangle I felt the give in the top cushion. The beize on the table looked well-worn and sure enough, as I rolled the white ball up and down the table, I could tell it was fast.

'Hey John, check the pro!' shouted one of his cronies. I removed the triangle and placed it in the ball tray. I flipped a coin.

'Tails.' said Kenny. It was heads. 'I'll break.' I said, picking up a cue from the rack on the wall. I raised the cue to my eye and looked along its length to check that it wasn't warped. The tip seemed better than the usual pub cue.

'See, check the pro John!' shouted the little twat from the bar. 'Actually that's my cue!' said his mate. 'But you can use it. We don't want you blaming the cue if you lose!Eh John?'

I chalked the cue. Addressed the white ball and gave it an almighty whack. I caught the triangle of red and yellow balls an absolute peach. The balls scattered all around the table. Five of them dropped into pockets. Three reds and two yellows. It was a cracking break. Two of the remaining four reds sat near a pocket, and the other two were wide open.

I glanced over at JK, who had lost his cocky grin. 'Reds' I said, chalking my cue. Two minutes later the game was over.

'Fuck me.He 9-balled him!' Said the guy who's cue I'd borrowed. JK threw him an evil look. 'Nice cue.' I said, replacing it in the rack 'Good game.' I said to Kenny, holding out my hand to shake his. He ignored the jesture and turned and wobbled back to the bar, slamming the bar-counter down as he went. To say there was an atmosphere would've been an understatement! I swigged the last of my pint. 'Cheers.' I said as I left.

I'm not a bad pool player, as I said. Mind you I'd even impressed myself then. There was one person that I'd definitely not impressed though.

I finished my kebab, threw the wrappings in the bin and stepped outside. It had turned quite chilly. I zipped up my jacket as I scanned the parked cars on the small car park in front of me. I hadn't seen the vehicle that Kenny had arrived in, but you didn't need to be a rocket scientist to work out which of these belonged to him.

The stand out vehicle in the car park was a big black Toyota twin cab truck. Extra large wheels, raised suspension, spotlights and go-faster stripes. Just in case I'd guessed completely wrongly, and in fact this wasn't your man's conveyance, the registration plate that became visible as I approached confirmed my suspicions. 335 JK. Tosser. What is it with people and their personal plates round here?

I carried on past his 'penis-enlargement' and hurried over to the convenience store, which according to my watch, was about to close. I got there in the nick of time. I bought an OS map of the local area, some high-energy drinks and all the 'C's' that I would need for a stake-out (crisps, chocky, chewing gum. Oh and my recent unhealthy addition to that list-cigarettes!) Returning to my hire car I put all my goodies in the boot. Unzipping my holdall I took out the tracker. I switched on the receiver and turned to channel 3. Screwing the base on the tiny transmitter connected the batteries and it gave out a steady beep, beep, beep.It was working fine. I turned off the receiver and tucking the transmitter in my sock I closed the boot. I walked towards the pub. As I neared JK's truck I scanned the car park Nobody around.At his truck I bent down as if to tie a shoe lace, and taking the transmitter from my sock I attatched it to his rear bumper. Seconds later I crossed the car park and walked into the Lion.

Chapter six

As I approached the bar I glanced to my right. No shocks there, fat boy was playing pool.

I pulled out a bar stool and sat at the bar, in the corner. Back to the wall, all entrances in view. I ordered a pint and picked up the pub newspaper. That was an improvement. 'The Mail.' John Kenny was no longer the landlord. He'd left, almost two years ago, under a bit of a cloud. Local gossip had it that he'd been on some sort of a fiddle. Owed the brewery money and had gone bankrupt.

Hence why I'd just stuck a tracker on his truck. He didn't live here any more. Mind you, the way he was strutting around the pool table, you would think he still owned the place. I had no idea where he was living now, but I intended to find out.

Sitting at the bar, sipping my pint, I had fat boy in my peripheral vision. I was sure he wouldn't recognise me. We'd only ever met a couple of times, the last time around 4 years ago. Besides, I looked totally different now. My hair was jet-black; I was very tanned, and was sporting a full moustache and beard. I looked like an Arab. I was meant to. I was glad that I hadn't shaved the lot off back at the B&B. I'd thought about it as the beard in particular had been itching like hell. Food had taken priority. I'd decided to shave later. Turned out to be a good move.

The barman was in his element. Every time one of the locals came in he was busy telling them all about the murderer that he'd served earlier that night. How he'd known there was something shifty about the guy. He'd been constantly looking at his mobile. Then his watch. Then the clock behind the bar. Yes, there had definitely been something dodgy about him.

'Of course' he was busy telling a new arrival 'When the cops arrested him we all thought it was for drink-driving. Not that he drank much here. He made half a lager last him nearly half an hour then he left. Cops were all over him like a rash. Turns out apparently he'd murdered some woman just outside the village, up near the Air Base.'

As I watched, JK necked most of a pint in order to accept a fresh one from one of his cronies. He also helped himself to a JD chaser from a tray.

'They took a statement from me.' The barman was off again. 'All the rooms are full, and at the Crown. Press mainly. They've been asking all sorts of questions aswell. I might be in the papers tomorrow.'

I ordered another pint, if nothing else it shut the barman up for a few minutes while he served me. Oh joy, some customers had just come in before last orders. They hadn't heard what had happened. Not yet. Off he went again 'Yes I served him . . .

My mind slipped back to my last visit to this pub. I'd been sitting where I was now. It was several months after the pool incident, but I could tell by the frosty reception from 'mein host' that he was still raw about it. This wouldn't have been my choice of venue, but a mate had wanted to meet me here. That friend was Jimmy Gordon. Jimmy had died, thanks to John Kenny.

Chapter seven

I'd first met Jimmy whilst on detatchment to the Falklands. He was RAF Regiment, but apart from that he was alright! We'd hit it off immediately and often met up for a beer or three whenever our paths crossed He'd rung me, right out of the blue, on the off-chance that I was around and available to have a few celebratory beers with him. He'd just been selected for promotion and was on his way to do a two week SNCO course, after which he would get his sergeants stripes and the nice posting to a training school which he'd applied for. He only had a few years left in the mob. He had a few family problems, mainly due to his kids, who by all accounts were a bloody nightmare. A nice cushy 9-5 job would mean he would be around more often 'To sort the little fuckers out!' as he'd so eloquently put it.

So here we were, at the Lion, celebrating Jimmy's promotion. I'd suggested having a pint here and then doing a pub-crawl of Bassett.I think I once read somewhere that Wooton Bassett was in the Guinness Book of Records for the town with the most pubs on a high street. Or something like that. Put it this way, there were plenty of other pubs to go to.

It didn't work out that way though. We got involved playing pool. As the night wore on and the pub got busier, we started playing doubles. Jimmy and I were proving difficult to beat.

As I said earlier, I'm a pretty good player. So, as it turned out was Jimmy. Our reasonable level of skill, combined with the run of the balls we were having meant we just couldn't loose. We could do no wrong, and we did some serious ass-kicking. JK was not amused.

At chucking-out time I suggested calling a cab or ringing my missus to come and collect us. We weren't pissed, but we'd had more than a few. Jimmy insisted he was fine to drive. In all honesty he probably was. However PC Plod and his little blow-in-the-bag trick disagreed. Don't get me wrong, I don't condone drinking and driving but Jimmy wasn't rolling drunk. He was just slightly over the limit.

As a civilian, if you get done for drinking and driving, you lose your licence and pay a fine. Slapped wrist, hole in the bank account and public transport for a year or so.

In the armed forces it doesn't work like that. After suffering all of the above he then had the joy of being marched in front of his CO. It could've been worse; he could have been Court Marshalled. 'Luckily' for him it was dealt with 'in house.'

Black Heart

Needless to say he wasn't promoted and he didn't get his cushy posting. Instead he got a punishment posting to Iraq.
He never came back.
At the magistrate's court I found out from a very reliable source that the police had been tipped off by the landlord of the Lion. He was doing his civic duty. Bollocks. If that was the case he would have stopped serving Jimmy. Or taken his car keys or called a taxi.
No, he was being a vindictive bastard, just because he lost a few games of pool. Through his actions he triggered a chain of events that resulted in a fine serviceman and a good friend losing his life. That was how I saw it anyway.
Looking at John Kenny now I can see a man who has drank at least half a dozen pints to my knowledge and God knows how many chasers. Wouldn't it be poetic justice if he got pulled by the police on his way home? I'd ring them, but I think they're a bit busy at the moment. No, I had plans for JK. Mind you the drinking and driving.Tragic accident? Mmm . . . .
Could be a good plan B. Plan A was good though.

Chapter eight

On the drive back from the Lion I mulled over the day's events. I'd come back to the UK to have a rest from death and killing. Within hours of my arrival I'd committed one murder and was already planning a second. What was happening to me? For over 20years I had been killing people for a living. I'd been trained to do it. I'd been trained very well and I was very good at it. I must be, or I wouldn't be here. But that was different, wasn't it? The people I'd killed were the enemy. When I first started my career in the army they were anyway. It was cut and dry. They held such and such position, we needed to take it. People got shot. Or we held a vantage point. They attacked and we fought them off. Again, people got shot. It wasn't anything personal. We were the goodies, they were the baddies. They were soldiers. Enemy soldiers. We were soldiers, but we were the good guys. We were fighting for Queen and country. I got payed; I even got decorated, for killing people. It was my job; it was what I signed up to do. The last few years had been different though. I was no longer in the army. I didn't wear a uniform. The people I killed didn't wear a uniform. The Americans have a good way to sum up what I do. Black Ops.

Somehow there is no black and white any more. The colours seem to have merged. Grey Ops would probably be a better description. OK my wife was shagging around. When I came home unexpectedly and caught her, was my response normal? I'm thinking the normal reaction would've been to dash up the stairs and kick off. It had been my first instinct. I'd fought off that instinct. Instead I had murdered her and framed her lover for her death. Now, hours later I was planning the death of a man for grassing a mate of mine to the cops. Fucking hell. Was I going mad? The way I saw it it was ok for me to kill people I'd never met. I didn't know them from Adam. But because of their uniform I had carte blanche to 'shoot them on sight'.
I pulled into the driveway of the B&B.
I needed a shave. Or a shrink, probably . . . .

Chapter nine

Back in my room I had a hot shower. I boiled the kettle so that I could have a decent shave. As I stood at the sink shaving off the bleeding annoying beard and tash, my thoughts went back to John Kenny. He had a few weaknesses that I planned to exploit. He was seriously overweight. He drank far too much. His idea of exercise was playing pool. He must have a dodgy ticker. I also happened to know that he was shit-scared of snakes. Apparently, according to the local gossip, he had been on holiday a few years back and as his wife had recalled, to the hilarity of the locals at the Lion, whilst at dinner one night at a restaurant in Majorca, he had apparently tipped a table-full of drinks over when he was approached by a guy offering to have your photo taken with a snake.

'A bleedin great snake!' as she'd put it.

In the morning I would phone my 'babysitter'.

I would go and get Monty.

Chapter ten

The next morning I got up at 06.00. I put on my trackies and trainers and slipped quietly out of the B&B. I ran along the dirt track and at every junction turned right. After about half an hour I passed through a cemetery and hit the main road and completing a circuit jogged about half a mile back to the B&B. After a quick shower I went down to breakfast. Over a good old full English I flicked through the papers. The missus had managed a small piece on page three. (No Charlie, leave it)

After breakfast, back in my room, I phoned the cop-shop. I was informed by the desk sergeant that the DI was catching up on some sleep but was expected in around lunchtime to continue questioning Gross.

I then rang my ops room to inform them of the B&B address. I was officially on compassionate leave and they did have my cell-phone number, but old habits die hard.

Next I rang Davey-boy. He answered on the third or forth ring

'Hey Charlie-barley you back in Blighty? When are we having a beer?'

'Well matey I was thinking of popping round yours about 7ish' I told him.

'Cool. I'll put my go-faster wheels on charge'.

'I'll see you at seven' I said and hung up.

Dave Wright was a para-plegic. He'd been hit by a roadside bomb in Helmand province. He'd lost both legs, one from the thigh and the other from the knee down. He'd also suffered severe facial scarring. I'd known Davey since basic training. We had literally gone through hell together. As our careers had progressed we had gone our separate ways, but we always tried to keep in touch. We then had a spate of meetings in the space of a few months, not always under great circumstances. Three funerals and a wedding. (You could make a film about that we'd joked at his wedding) Squaddie humour.

Yes, three funerals of friends killed in action in as many months. At the last one, an ex SNCO of ours known as Skippy, Davey informed me that he was getting married. It was a rush job. Emma, his girlfriend, was pregnant. Not that they wouldn't have got married eventually anyway. God they'd been together since high school. No, to keep her mum and dad happy they wanted to 'Tie-the-knot', before the bump started to show. Also they wanted a 'pad' (married quarter) Davey wanted to get Em settled before she had the baby. It was due in September and he was due to go back to Afghanistan just in time for Christmas.

He hadn't told her that yet. They had contacted all of the local registry offices and put their names down in case of a

cancellation. Davey had a call the morning of Skippy's funeral to say that they could get married the following Tuesday at 11am. Talk about short notice. Six days to organise your wedding. Well if anyone could do it Em could.
'You've just saved me a stamp. Or actually more likely a text'. Said Davey over a pint at Skippy's wake. I told him that I didn't know if I could make it.
'You bleedin better mate, you're the best man!'
'Give me loads of notice why don't you' I told him
'Fucks sake Charlie, I only found out myself about four hours ago!'
Luckily I had a good boss at the time. He let me stay on after the funeral to be Davey's best man. It was a great do, concidering the short notice. The registry office was pretty full. Even more people turned up for the evening bash at Davey's local, The Barrel. Davey and Em had a lot of friends. Either that or everyone had turned up for the good nosh and the award winning 'loopy-juice' that they brew there. Everyone seemed pretty pissed to me. Happy days.

Chapter eleven

The next time that I saw Davey was about 18 months later. He had been medivaced back from Afghanistan and was at the John Radcliffe Hospital. He had now been transferred from the ICU to a ward and was in a stable condition. I'd received a call from a very distressed Emma about 10 days earlier, but just couldn't get back at the time. As I walked down the ward to his bed I was trying to think of something to say. I mean, what do you say to your best mate who's just had both his legs blown off?
I settled for 'If you're not going to wear those nice Nike trainers of yours any more, can I have them?' (More squaddie humour) 'Fuck off, I can wear them on me prosthetics when I get them' was Davey's reply. We hugged. He was crying on my shoulder as Em and their kiddy arrived. Turns out the soppy twats had named the nipper Charlie, after me. My eyes filled up. Fucks sake, why Davey?
This had all been about 8 months ago. Davey had gone through some real 'lows' before he started to come to terms with his injuries. According to Em he had spoken about topping himself several times. The really low point had come when the army de-mobbed him. I phoned him at the time and told him to look on the bright side.

Black Heart

'Think of the compensation cheque' I'd said. We both knew he would get a pittance.

One day, about a month after he'd been de-mobbed, I was waiting to board a flight at Brize Norton. I remembered it was nearly Davey's birthday so I gave him a call. I couldn't believe the change in him. He'd decided that he was going into training for the 2012 para-olympics. Apparently he'd watched a documentary about a South African guy who had legs made out of carbon fibre or Teflon or whatever, but he was so fast that he could beat able-bodied athletes and that they wanted him banned.

'So what are you going in for?' I asked him.

'The wheelchair steeplechase!' he said, laughing his tits off. God I loved that guy. At least he had stopped all that suicide talk.

Chapter twelve

I went out to the hire car. I popped the boot and took out the receiver and its detatchable antenna. I also got the OS map that I'd bought from the convenience store. I got in the car and, assembling the telemetry, I put it on the front passenger seat. It had a maximum range of 30 miles. That would be plenty. JK wouldn't live too far away. I switched it on and heard the reassuring beep, beep, beep. This system had been designed for tracking hawks and falcons. I'd first seen one used by a mate of mine who kept birds of prey. I'd been out hawking with him a few times. It had been great fun. I was glad I was in good shape because when his birds went after their prey, shit did they move. Amazed and impressed as I was with the birds, it was the telemetry that had impressed me most. I had to have a set and had bought one off the internet. This system was capable of taking me up to 30 miles in a straight line to the exact tree a bird was sitting in. That kind of accuracy wouldn't be necessary. All I needed to do was work out roughly where the signal was coming from and drive over there. Once I got to the right road or street, I would be able to see his truck as I drove along. Unless of course it was in a garage or parked out of sight behind his house. Sitting in the car now and moving the antenna from left to right, the signal was coming from almost straight ahead of me. I could tell by adjusting the volume that the transmitter was no more than 2 or 3 miles away.

I unfolded the map. I located the B&B where I was now sat in my car. The main road in front of me was the A3102 Left would take me to my house, right to Wooton Bassett. Once in Bassett the road, which was always heading due north from me eventually came to a roundabout and split in three directions. One of the roads led out of the town constantly curving to the left.

About a mile and a half outside the town there was a small housing estate consisting of two or three roads with several cul-de-sacs leading from them. From the scale of the map that estate was about 3 miles. As the Hawk flies.

I re-folded the map. Force of habit. I started the car and pulled out onto the road.

Passing through Bassett I came to the roundabout. I took the left turn. I watched the trip meter on the speedo. Somewhere about here. Yep there it was the left turn I was looking for. I was very close according to the beeping coming from the seat beside me. OK now I had a choice, left or right. I tried right but it was a dead end cul-de-sac. Turning round I drove back to the junction and went straight across. 100 metres along the road there was another cul-de-sac on my right. As I turned in the telemetry was beeping almost off the scale. I switched it off. Dead ahead of me, reversed up a steep driveway of a semi-detatched 2 or 3 bedroomed house, right in the corner of the cul-de-sac, sat a black truck. 335 JK. Behind the house were open fields. In the distance I could see the main road I'd just turned off to come onto the estate. Perfect. Your days are numbered Mr Kenny.

Chapter thirteen

I drove back to the B&B, stopping on the way to buy the 'I' newspaper. I enjoy the crosswords and word-ladders and had plenty of time to kill.

I must have nodded off doing the crossword as I was awakened at 2pm by my phone ringing. It was the DI; he was ringing to ask me to come down to the station to see if I could pick Gross out of a line-up. I told him that it was doubtful as I hadn't really seen him, just his vehicle. Anyway, to show willing, I said I would be there in half an hour.

At the station I was, as I'd predicted, unable to identify Gross. It turned out not to be a problem as one of my neighbours (Nosey Norman as we'd called him) had already positively ID'd him. He'd made a statement that he'd seen Gross arrive at our house at about 5pm the evening of the murder. He'd seen my wife let him in through the front door. He'd been carrying a take away and a few bottles of wine. He also said that he had seen him drive off in a hurry just before 7.30pm. He was sure of the time as he was in the kitchen making a cup of tea before Coronation Street started. Gross had come out of our front door, dashed to his car and drove off in a hurry towards Wooton Basset.

Shortly after that he had seen me walk up the driveway. He hadn't recognised me at first though as I looked Different. 'You do look totally different minus all that facial hair' said the DI as I followed him to his office. Once seated he proceeded to fill me in on the case. Gross had been charged with the murder of my wife. He was going to appear in court later that day. The prosecution were going to oppose bail and have him remanded in custody. The evidence against him was overwhelming. So much so, that his own lawyer had told him to plead guilty. 'He can't deny he was at the scene. We have eye-witnesses. His DNA is everywhere. Semen on the bedclothes and, well, you know, on and in your wife' (he blushed.) 'His fingerprints are on the wine bottles and glasses. His tie was used to strangle your wife. We've checked his and your wifes phone records and know that they'd been in regular contact for some time. We even have a record of gross receiving a call on his cell-phone at your address at 7.16pm last night. It goes on and on. If he's got any sense he will take his lawyer's advice and plead guilty. If he pleads not guilty he's going down for life.

Plead guilty to manslaughter due to diminished responsibility he might get 10 or 12 years and be out in half that.'

Chapter fourteen

I pulled out of the police station car park. It was 3.30pm. I wasn't due at Davey's until 7pm. He lived about an hour away in Kidlington, near Oxford. I decided to go and check out the lie of the land behind John Kenny's house. I headed back out on the main drag out of Wooton Bassett, passing the turn off to his housing estate, I continued for about ¾ of a mile. As the road started to veer to the left I could see in the distance the cluster of houses in my rear view mirror. I pulled into a lay-by. I popped the boot and took out my 'bins'. I locked the car and jumped over a low fence into a large field. There wasn't much in the way of crops but the roadside hedge provided cover from any passing motorists. Bringing the bins up to my eyes I scanned the distant houses, looking for his truck. Due to the lay of the land I couldn't see it. No matter. I knew his was one of a small cluster of properties to the left. I noticed a line of power cables stretching from the road, across the fields behind the estate and heading off into the distance. If I could identify the telegraph pole that was nearest to JK's house, it would give me a good marker against the sky-line to head for in the dark. I walked back to the car, fired up the engine and doing a U-turn, headed back towards WB. I took the right turn into the estate and stopped near to the turning into

JK's cul-de-sac without actually going in. I counted the telegraph poles. The forth from the main road was smack bang behind his house. I turned the car around and set off back the way I'd just come. As I passed the lay-by where I'd previously parked I slowed down. I scanned both sides of the road. Within a few hundred metres I found what I was looking for. Just up ahead, on the left, was a dirt track. I turned in. About 100 metres up the track I came to a couple of abandoned farm sheds. Perfect. I could park my car here when I came to pay Mr Kenny a visit.
I pulled into the second of the sheds in order to reverse out and drive back to the main road. I turned left and headed off to Davey's.

Chapter fifteen

I pulled up outside Davey's at just before 7pm. As I walked to the front door I noticed the adaptions to the property-wheelchair ramp, handrails etc. I rang the doorbell. Moments later the door opened and Em threw herself at me, hugging me and kissing me.
'Oi, calm down gal, I'm a married man' (I wasn't any more actually!)
'Put my Missus down you slag' Davey had wheeled up to the door behind Em. He sat there smiling, little Charlie on his lap.
'He's getting big isn't he?' I said, untangling myself from Em and going over to give Davey a hug. Little Charlie stared at me and grinned.
'God he's got teeth' I said.
'Yea and he's crawling and getting into all sorts of shit. Do you want him?' Said Davey
'What's a guy got to do to get a beer around here?' I complained.
'Squaddies!' Sighed Em, squeezing past us en-route to the kitchen. 'Wobblies?' she shouted, head in the fridge.
'What else?' Davey and I shouted, almost in unison. Wobbly was the nickname for Warsteiner, a german beer served on all the British bases in Germany. Or rather was—we don't have any bases left in Germany.

Following a lovely roast dinner, a bottle of red wine and several more wobblies I told them about Sally. Well there was no point mentioning it earlier and spoiling their dinner. Em surprised me by being quite tearful and hugging me. I hadn't thought them to be that friendly towards each other. 'More beer?' said Davey. His way of cheering the mood. 'Only if I can crash for the night' I said 'Course mate, Em's already made up the spare bed for you.' While Em was busy bathing the nipper and getting him off to bed Davey and I sank a few more beers. He told me that he'd been doing well at basketball and was shit hot at throwing the javelin. He'd been making waves in the right places and apparently had been getting noticed. He'd been short listed to trial for the London 2012 Olympics. Good lad.

By about 11.30 we were all pretty pissed. (Legless, Davey had called himself, nice to see him coming to terms with his disability and joking about it).

We called it a night and drunkenly made our way to bed.

Chapter sixteen

What the fuck. Was I dreaming? No I wasn't. Someone was sucking my cock. I opened my eyes. 'Em What the?' She silenced me with her mouth over mine, at the same time impaling herself on me. 'Mmm . . .' I pushed her lips away from mine and whispered 'What are you doing? What if Davey wakes up?'
Em continued to rise and fall on me as she said 'He won't wake up, he's been drinking with you. He couldn't do that before and he certainly can't now. Besides, one of his pain-killers knocks him out and I gave him two.'
'Em this is wrong we can't . . .' she smothered my mouth with hers again. Pushing her head away I continued 'Em, Davey is my best mate.'
'Do you know how long it is since I had a cock inside me?' She was very warm and moist and continued to work up and down.
'Em I . . .'
She cut me off again. 'The fucking Taliban didn't just blow his legs off you know. Oh he's still got a cock but he doesn't do anything apart from piss with it.'
'Em, look he's still my best mate. We can't do this.'
'You didn't say that the last time we made love' she was gyrating and squeezing.

'Come on Em I was drunk. We both were. It was New Years Eve. Davey was away and it just happened. This is different. You're married now and you have a kid.'

'Yes Charlie I have a kid. And whose kid, do you suppose he is?'

'What?' The kid was mine? Surely not. God she was still riding my cock.

'Does he look remotely like Davey? No he doesn't. He's the spitting image of you. Why the fuck do you think I named him Charlie?'

'Oh my God. But surely not, we only had a one night stand, I mean . . .'

'Trust me Charlie, I know. A mother knows. Do you want to do a paternity test?' All the time she was moving up and down my cock. I also couldn't remember the last time I'd had sex. I just gave in to the moment and returned her thrusts. When she came I had to stick my hand over her mouth. We lay together in silence. The reality of what she had just told me began to sink in. Jesus, Charlie was my kid.

Chapter seventeen

I went to the bathroom for a pee. Returning to my room I expected Em to have gone back to her own bed. Wrong. She had turned on the bedside light and was sitting cross-legged, stark naked in the middle of the bed smoking a joint.

'Fucks sake Em, what's that all about?'

'We get it for Davey, it helps with the pain. Or rather it used to. He's fine on it unless he's on a downer, which is most of the time. I probably smoke more of the damn stuff than him. It's the only way that I can get through the day sometimes. I don't know how much longer I can do this Charlie. Davey is just getting worse.'

'What do you mean? He seemed fine to me.'

'Oh he was fine tonight. That's because you were here Charlie. He's constantly talking about topping himself. He's asked me dozens of times to help him. I have to hide his drugs up out of his reach, like a kid. Once I thought about going out for the day and leaving them where he could get to them. God I could do with the Life Insurance money.'

'Life Insurance?'

'Yes we took out a £100, 000 policy on him when we knew little Charlie was on the way. What with Davey going off to Afghanistan and all that.'

'Em, I don't think a war zone would be covered. I also doubt very much if the fuckers would pay out if he topped himself. Trust me. Insurance companies are great at taking your payments but you try claiming for something.'

'Suppose so.' She said passing me the spliff. Surprisingly I found myself accepting it from her and taking a long toke, inhaling it deeply. I had never touched any drugs in my life. It would've been the end of my career. All military personnel and government agents are subject to random drugs testing. One strike and you're out. Ironically the class 'c' drugs such as cannabis, which are comparatively safe, are the worst to take. They can be detected up to a month after use, whereas your dodgy class A's such as heroin are almost untraceable after 24 hours. And we wonder why all our prisons, and on release society in general, is full of 'smack-heads.'

'Hey you junky, save some for me!' Said Em. I hadn't realised but I'd smoked the whole joint. 'Don't worry,' said Em 'I'll skin another one.' I watched, in fascination as she rolled another joint. 'What exactly am I smoking' I asked as I took a toke on the second spliff.

'This is squidgy black' said Em, who then went on to give me an idiot's guide to weed.

'So what is it supposed to do?' I asked 'Apart from that stupid grin on your face?' Said Em.

Being a complete novice at this, it wasn't long before I had the 'giggles'. 'Give me another poke' I said. 'You mean toke' said Em. 'Or do you actually want another poke?' That was it, I started giggling uncontrollably. I was rolling round the bed laughing so much that my ribs hurt. 'That's enough for you. I don't want you throwing a 'whitey' said Em smiling

'A wh . . . .' I was cut off mid-word as the bedroom door flew inward.

Chapter eighteen

Davey was leopard crawling unsteadily towards us, using his one knee and both elbows, all the time keeping the Browning 9mm pointed at us in a double-handed grip.

The stupid grins vanished from mine and Emmas faces.

Davey wasn't smiling either.

'Having fun are we?' Hissed Davey. Not any more I thought. As Davey neared us he positioned his left elbow on the bed as he attempted to lever himself up.

Now! He was momentarily unbalanced and had taken his eyes off of us as he tried to negotiate his way up onto the bed. With one movement I had taken the weapon from his grasp and with a flick of the wrist had slammed it into the side of his head. He dropped like a stone to the floor. Em threw her arms around me 'Is he ok?' 'He'll be fine. I just gave him a slap.' I disengaged myself from her and slid off the bed.

I shook him. Nothing. I felt for a pulse. Nothing. Shit, I'd caught him a bit sweeter than intended. I began CPR.

'What are you doing?' Asked Em. 'What does it look like? Phone for an ambulance'

'Yeh right.' 'What's the Emergency madam?' 'Oh nothing I was shagging my husband's best mate and he caught us and pulled a gun on us, so my lover killed him!'

I sat back on my heels. The CPR wasn't working anyway. I tried to clear my head of the booze and drugs. I sat on the bed and lit a cigarette. Fuck fuck fuck! I'd just killed my best mate. No, I'd just killed my best mate in front of his wife that I'd just fucked. Em put her arms around me. 'I'm so sorry Em I truly didn't mean to hit him that hard. He had a gun. I was pissed and stoned. I honestly didn't mean to kill him.'

'The gun wasn't loaded Charlie. He's been suicidal for months. I hid his ammo. Looks like he found a way to commit suicide after all. I think what just happened is what Davey would have wanted.' I stubbed out my cigarette and lit another one. Shit I couldn't think straight. 'Em can you go and make some strong black coffee, I need to get my head clear. We need to do something, and quickly, otherwise they will know the body has been moved. If we do this right we can make it look like an accident. Do you really think Davey wanted this to happen?'

'I don't know Charlie, not for sure. It's just a feeling. Knowing Davey, how he's been recently. He put you in a situation. He knew that. He knows what you are capable of. He pushed you into a position that required a split second reaction. You weren't to know that his gun wasn't loaded. He knew it wasn't. He knew what might happen. Actually yes. I do think this is what Davey wanted. I truly mean that, I'm not just saying it to make you feel better. I'll go and make that coffee now.'

Chapter nineteen

I turned Davey's head to one side. There was no blood, just a lump on his temple that had started to bruise. I quickly got dressed. I picked up the 9mm and made it safe, even though it wasn't loaded, force of habit. Stuffing the weapon in the waistband of my jeans, I got a hold of Davey under the arm pits and dragged him out of the bedroom, across the landing and propped him up against the wall at the top of the stairs. I went downstairs and took a few swigs of the coffee that Em had made. 'Ok Em, listen carefully. If we do this right it will appear to be nothing more than a tragic accident. It will be an ambulance crew or para-medic. A doctor to sign the death certificate. No real need for the cops to go sniffing around. The Coroner will most likely determine the cause of death as accidental. When Davey goes up and down the stairs he does so on his bum, yeah?' Em nodded agreement. 'Ok, that nest of tables. Get the smallest one and put it there, at the bottom of the stairs. Then get something to put on it. A plant would be good.' I went back up the stairs. Gripping Davey around the hips I dragged him down the stairs on his back, his head bouncing off each step. Half a dozen steps from the bottom I placed his right leg, the longest one, through the stair

rails. I gave him a swift kick to the opposite hip, enough to bruise. I then pulled his arms so that he ended up head-down at the bottom of the stairs. Holding him up off the ground, I kicked over the table and plant and dropped Davey onto the resulting mess.
I took a few strides into the open plan lounge/diner and surveyed my handywork.
Hopefully, when the emergency services arrived it would appear to them that Davey had been on his way down the stairs, had lost his balance and slid down on his arse until his leg got caught, flipping him over and causing him to land head-first on the table at the bottom of the stairs.
'Will it work?' Asked Em.
'It's all we've got.' I said. 'So what now.Ring for an ambulance?' She asked.
'No. Now we wait.' I said. 'How long for?'
I looked at my watch. It was a little after 01.30.
'As long as possible. If we dial 999 at about 8am. Half an hour for them to get here. He would've been in that position for the best part of 7 hours.'
Em was looking a bit pale so I didn't go into detail about rigor mortis, or the blood pooling in his head, thus establishing how long he had been lying there.

Black Heart

'Come on.' I took Em's hand and led her to the kitchen. There we sat, mainly in silence, sipping coffee. At one point Em had said she wanted to take a shower to freshen up. I'd told her no, we needed to look like we'd just got up when the ambulance arrived. It was a long night.

Chapter twenty

At 08.00 Em made the 999 call. The ambulance arrived at 08.12. As I heard the approaching sirens I turned Davey over and dragged him off the stairs. I answered the door. Em was in the kitchen, trying to calm little Charlie, who was screaming his head off. She was doing that jiggle-on-the-hip thing that women do whilst making him a bottle.

The medics rushed over to Davey and quickly established that he was dead.

'Who found the body?' One of them asked. 'I did.' I replied
'Is this how you found him?'
'No, he was lying face down on the stairs. I dragged him off the stairs and turned him over to check for a pulse. There was no pulse and I could tell by how cold and stiff he was that he'd been here for some time.'
'Quite so. Are you a medic sir?'
'No Armed Forces. I've seen my share of corpses. We served together.'
'Ah, is that what happened to his legs?' 'Yep.Roadside bomb.'
A few minutes later PC Plodd arrived and stood at the front door chatting to the ambulance crew. He glanced over at the body which had been loosely covered with a green sheet. I went over to

Black Heart

the computer desk and flipped open the address book. Under 'M' I found what I was looking for. I phoned Em's mum. We'd met before. I told her what had happened and she said she was on her way. The copper came over and told me that a doctor was on his way. The ambulance crew were needed on another call. He asked if I could stay. I told him that I'd just phoned Em's mother and that yes I would stay, at least until she arrived. He flipped open his notebook and said 'I just need to take a few details for our records sir.' I told him what he wanted to know. He thanked me and left. Shortly after that the doctor arrived, closely followed by Jill, Em's mother. I guided Jill through to the kitchen, shielding her view of the body which the doc was busy examining.

My cell-phone buzzed and vibrated in my pocket. I took it out and read the text. It was just one word.

Peregrine.

I pressed reply then typed in 'Falcon' and pressed send. 30 seconds later my phone rang. The screen said 'witheld'. No shocks there. I unlocked the kitchen door and stepped out into the back garden. I took the call. 'Charlie, how are you?' 'I'm good Dimitri, and you?'

'I'm good also. Can we meet?' 'Yes.' I said 'Bravo in 2hours.'

'Would Alpha be better then?' 'No Bravo is best for me. I'm just a bit tied up at the moment.' I said.'Ok Bravo at 11. 00.' the line went dead.

I had no idea what he wanted. I did know one thing though. Dimitri didn't make social calls.

I went back into the house. Quickly showered and changed. Gathering all my kit together I went back downstairs. I gave Em a hug and told her that I would give her a call later. Little Charlie was nice and calm now, in his Nan's arms.

'Oh Em, the other reason I came was to get Monty. Can I . . . .?'

'You know where he is. Help yourself.' I went over to his tank and lifted the lid.

'Hey my boy you've grown.' It was probably a year or more since I'd seen him. He was now close on 6ft long and as thick as my arm. Monty was a python.Probably 5 or 6 years old now. He still had a lot of growing to do but he was plenty big enough for what I had in mind. I lowered him into the sack and pulled the draw-string tight. Slinging him over my shoulder I picked up my kit and made my way through the lounge, which was now full of neighbour's, undertakers and God knows who else. I squeezed past them all to the front door. I loaded everything into the boot and took out my sat-nav. I typed in my start co-ordinates and the post code of Bravo, my destination.

Black Heart

As I waited for the gadget to work out a route I lit a cigarette. I sat and thought about recent events. Fuck me two stiffs in as many days. Not to mention whatever Dimitri had in mind. Oh and JK still had to get his. I felt like I was starring in my own episode of Midsommer Murders. And I hadn't finished yet. Not by a long chalk.

The sat-nav had done its thing. Approximate journey time to my destination was 1hr 10minutes. Perfect. I fastened my seat belt, stubbed out my cig, started the engine and drove off to my meeting with the Russian.

Chapter twenty one

Dimitri was a dodgy geezer, to say the least. He'd been 'turned' by the CIA and had worked as a double agent in Russia during the 'cold war'. When the Berlin wall came down and we all became best buddies with 'Boris' Dimitri had been given a new identity and a new life in the USA.

Not one to settle for a quiet life Dimitri had began working with the FBI the ATF and various other agencies in the fight against organised crime. In particular the so called 'Russian Mafia'.

The last I'd heard of Dimitri was that he was under suspicion of being 'in the pocket' of a very powerful Russian mobster known as 'Red.'

Thousands of hours of surveillance and countless dollars had been invested into bringing Red to justice. But, somehow, he always seemed to be one step ahead of the authorities.

As the saying goes 'every man has his price.' The Russian mafia had a lot of money to throw around. Bribing the local bobby to turn a blind eye was not the way things were done these days.

Black Heart

I got changed into my swimming trunks. I put my clothes into the locker and attatched the key to my wrist using the elastic band it was attatched to. I went through to the pool and immediately received a large whistle-blast from the pool attendant for running and diving into the pool-apparently a double fault. I surfaced and raised my hand to the jobs-worth by way of an apology. Fucks sake, no running, no diving, no snorkling. I'm surprised you're allowed to swim.

'I see you're making friends and influencing people' said Dimitri with a grin. 'I almost didn't recognise you with the black hair and tan. How are you my friend?'

'I'm fine Dimitri. You should've seen me yesterday. I had a full beard and moustache!'

'I'm guessing Afghanistan. Or should I not ask' said Dimitri.

'Ask me no questions and I vill tal you no lays.' I said in my best Russian accent. We swam to the end of the pool and sat on the edge with our feet dangling in the water. The reason that we usually chose to meet in a swimming pool was simple. It's nigh on impossible to 'wear a wire!'

'I'm sorry to hear about your wife' said Dimitri. Fuck me, news travelled fast. If he mentioned Davey I'd freak out!

'Charlie I will get straight to the point. Associates of mine would like a certain someone to, well, er, disappear. Disappear permanently.' 'So why can't you deal with it?' I asked.

'It's very complicated my friend. Sure I could 'deal with it' as you put it. But, I have to be completely above suspicion. In fact I will be several thousand miles away at the time of the 'disappearance.'

'Who, where, and how much?' I asked him.

'I will answer those questions in reverse order Charlie. I have been authorised to pay you $500, 000. This will be in the form of $100, 000 in advance. The balance to be paid exactly one year after the er 'disappearance.' The body must not be found. The where is up to you. The subject will be arriving at Heathrow from Moscow tomorrow. He will be staying in the London area for three days. Before I say any more, are you interested?'

'500, 000 pounds, Not dollars, and I'm still interested.'

Dimitri grinned. 'I knew you would say that Charlie.'

'So, assuming I make this person disappear, who is going to be looking for me?'

'I can assure you Charlie that nobody from the FBI, ATF, CIA or any other US government agency is going to miss him.

Although they would not, could not sanction his demise, they certainly won't be upset by his disappearance.'

'Dimitri I didn't ask you who wouldn't be looking for me. Who will be looking for me?'

'Just some Russians.' Said Dimitri. 'Just some Fucking Russians? Oh no problem then, eh?'

'Charlie, if you carry this out with your usual skill and efficiency, you will have nothing to worry about. You have absolutely no connection to the target. The Russians are going to be looking in completely the wrong direction, at all the wrong people. That is why I need to be in New York, with some dodgy Russians who will inadvertently provide me with an alibi.'

'So who is paying me to do this hit?' I asked him. 'I can't tell you that Charlie.'

'Ok Dimitri, let me put it another way. If, in a year's time I don't get my 400k, who do I come looking for?'

'That will have to be me then.' Said Dimitri.

'Let us hope it doesn't come to that then eh my friend?'

I dived into the water and swam to the other end of the pool. I got out and headed to the changing rooms.
In the locker room I was sat on a bench, leaning forward tying the laces on my trainers. A black holdall was placed at my feet. I looked up at Dimitri, who smiled 'Dos vidanya commrade' he said as he walked away.

Chapter twenty two

In the hire car I placed the holdall on the front passenger seat and unzipped it. Inside was a tan folder. I lifted it out. Underneath were four £25k bundles. I smiled to myself. Dimitri had known I would want pounds, not dollars. I opened the folder. Inside were several 10"x 8" surveillance photos of a rather ordinary looking middle-aged man. Underneath were a few photos of a very mean looking character. The single sheet of type-written paper had on it Photos 1-5 Vladimir Checkov. Photos 6 and 7 Sergey Karpov (Checkov's bodyguard)

Thanks for that little surprise Dimitri. There followed an itinerary of Checkov's flight details, where he would be staying and places he was expected to go, or was likely to go.

Likely to go. That was no use to me. The only definites were his flight details and the hotel he was booked into tomorrow night. Everything else was speculation. Guesswork based on intelligence. Typical yanks. Ok Dimitri was Russian but he was getting more like a yank the longer he worked with them.

The way I saw this was simple. There were only two definates. His flight itinerary and the fact that he was staying in the Barbican Hotel tomorrow night. The flights were of no use to me.

You would have to be crazy to try and make a hit on someone at an airport. Too much security and too many cameras. I lit a cigarette and sat thinking for a few minutes.

That left the hotel. The problem was not just getting past his bodyguard and killing Checkov. I also had to get his body out of the hotel and make it 'disappear.'

By the time I'd finished my ciggy I had the rough formulation of a plan in my head.

I phoned Em. 'Hiya. How are you? Is your mum still there?'

'I'm fine Charlie. No my mum's just left. She's gone to work. She said she would come back later and stay the night if I needed the company. Why?'

'Do you think you can put her off without too much shit? I was thinking of coming back tonight.' 'Sure Charlie. You or my mother? A bit of a no-brainer really. I'll ring her and put her off. What time will you be here? As in do you want me to cook?'

'I'll be there at about 7.30. Don't worry about cooking, I'll pick up a Chinese on the way back. What's the chinky like near your place?'

'It's pretty good especially the Singapore Vermicelli.'

'Ok madam tonight dinner is on me. See you at 7.30-8.00.'

Chapter twenty three

As I drove towards London I took out my 'work phone' and powered it up. No messages. I scrolled through my contacts 'till I got to Frank. I speed-dialled him.
'Frank my man, how are you?'
'I'm great Charlie, what are you after?' I told him what I needed. We haggled over the price, as usual. Concidering the short notice I think I got a good deal.
'I'm on my way now. I'm estimating I should be with you between 4 and 5pm. I'll confirm nearer the time.' 'Ok buddy, I'll be ready.' He said. I hung up. I had plenty of time until our meet, so I pulled into the next motorway services. I went to the gents and had a pee. On the way back to the car I got a coffee to take away. Tipping half a dozen sachets of sugar into the styrofoam bucket as I approached the hire car I noticed one of those jobs-worth car park attendants entering my vehicle details into one of those hand-held electronic gizmos that they carry. Probably because they can't write. Fuck. It's no big deal but I just don't like leaving any kind of trail. The car park was full of cameras as well.Fucking 'Big Brother.'
I knew one thing; I would be changing vehicles asap. I got into the car and continued my journey. I'd made good time, so just

outside London I pulled into a large 'Retail City' I parked outside B&Q and went into the store. I had several items on my shopping list.

As I approached the front of the queue at the check-out I checked my watch and phoned Frank. I told him that I would be at our usual RV in 45minutes. I told him to make sure he wasn't late as I wouldn't be able to wait due to all the nazzis (traffic wardens) I unloaded my trolly-full of goodies into the car boot and headed off to meet Frank.

As I approached Bakers Street tube station I slowed to a crawl. Yep there was Frank. He hadn't seen me. Why would he, I was in a hire car. I flashed my lights and indicated left. (That's not strictly true, what I actually did was squirt water on my windscreen and then set off the windscreen wipers, then I flashed my lights and indicated to pull in. Is it just me? Or do they need to standardise wipers, indicators etc?!) I stopped just long enough for Frank to jump in next to me. 'Long time no see. Been away Charlie? I know, don't ask!'

I'd dealt with Frank many times over the years. Yes, I'm sure he'd supplied lots of dodgy people lots of dodgy stuff, but I personally liked the bloke. As I plodded slowly through the heavy traffic he passed me the credit card I'd asked for. I checked it over, it looked great. I put it in my top pocket.

Next he took out the Glock 9mm complete with silencer and full magazine. Keeping the weapon low in the passenger seat footwell he removed the mag, cocked and released the workings to make the weapon safe then re-fitted the magazine. 'Looks fine to me Frank.' I said, reaching under my seat to retrieve the envelope of crisp £50 notes. I handed it to him. He had a quick look and then stuck the envelope into his jacket pocket. 'I trust you Charlie.'
He said as I pulled over to let him jump out. 'Laters.' I said as I pulled away back into the traffic. I didn't know it then but I'd be seeing him again very soon.
I fought my way through several lanes of traffic and headed back north to Em.
Em and little Charlie actually. No Em and my son to be precise. Fucking hell, I was definitely getting soft in my old age!

Chapter twenty four

I tapped on the door of Em's at just after 7.30pm armed with the promised Chinese take-away. She opened the door and gave me a big hug. I could tell the day's events were still playing on her mind. She looked . . . 'Stressed' I suppose was the best description. We ate our meal in an awkward silence, little Charlie was in his play pen munching on the free prawn crackers that came with the meal. Em hardly ate anything and I wasn't as hungry as I thought I was. Em tidied the left over food away. 'I've put it in the fridge. You know what Chinese food is like, we'll be starving in an hour!
If so we can 'nuke' it, if not it won't be wasted, the chickens will have it.' While Em pottered about clearing up plates etc I nipped out to the car. I counted out 10 grand and put it in my overnight kit. I grabbed Monty and locked the car. Back inside the house I took Monty out of his sack and hung him over my neck. I wanted to spend some time with him and get him used to being handled again. Em came through from the kitchen. She looked a bit concerned when she saw Monty. 'Don't worry; I won't let him loose while Charlie's about. He's a bit big for Monty anyway.'
'No it's fine I'm going to bath Charlie and put him to bed now, so it's not a problem.'

'Can you remember when Davey last fed Monty?' I asked her.
'Oh it was only a few days ago. He had a rabbit. I'm just going to sort the laddo out I'll be back soon.'
I decided to put Monty back in his tank, just in case he decided to have a dump-that could be smelly. I'd had him for 5 or 6 years now. I say I'd had him. Davey'd had him for half that time. His was a more stable set up. I spent too much time away from home. Besides, my Missus had hated him. I'd found him in a pallet of cargo on an RAF Hercules. I was flying back from Jungle Training in Belize. I'd done 100's of hours as a passenger on 'Hercs'. They are not exactly built for comfort. You sit along the side of the aircraft, strapped in like sardines in a glorified deck chair, surrounded by huge great 8ft high pallets of freight. As a seasoned traveller on these aircraft I'd found a much better way to endure these 12hr plus legs. What I did was 'suss out'a likely looking pallet of freight, in this case a pallet-full of empty cargo nets on its way back to RAF Lyneham. After take-off, as soon as I'd got the 'thumbs-up' from the 'loadie' that it was ok to move about the aircraft, I climbed up onto the top of the stack of nets. I took an aircraft strop with me to act as a seat belt. (That way I wouldn't be woken up and told to go back to my seat in the event of us encountering any turbulence.)I got myself comfy, using my cam jacket as a pillow, I clipped the strop to the net. Passed it

over my waist and attatched it to the net on the other side of me, happy days, I could now sleep through the entire journey. A few hours out of Lyneham, I was half awake, contemplating trudging my way to the back of the aircraft to take a pee. That's when I felt something move in the small of my back. My first thought had been tarantula; I wasn't too keen on them. I unclipped the strop and looked into the bundle of nets. I could see a snake peering at me through the mesh. We'd had an extensive training course on all the snakes and creepy-crawlies that we were likely to encounter in the jungle, so I was fairly confident that it wasn't venomous, even so I dug my NI gloves out of my battle kit. Putting a glove on my right hand I managed to pull the snake from the net. I was fairly certain it was a young python hence I called him Monty. I got out my mess tins and putting him in one I closed the other on top of him. That would keep him, and me safe until I could get him positively identified.

Chapter twenty five

Upstairs Em was bathing little Charlie, I could hear him gurgling and splashing.

I took out my phone and 'googled' the Barbican Hotel. I phoned the number and reserved a twin room with disabled facilities for the following night. I hung up as Em came into the lounge with her son.Correction, our son. She leaned towards me with him and said 'Give Uncle Charlie a kiss night-night.' He grinned at me and gave me a rather slavery kiss.

'I fancy a beer, is it ok to' 'Sure' interupted Em 'get one for me too, I'll be back in a minute.' I got two wobblies from the fridge, opened them and went back to the lounge. While I waited for Em to get Charlie settled into bed I rang the DI for an update on the case. I had to keep up the appearance of a grieving husband. The DI told me that as expected Gross had been remanded in custody until his trial date which had been set for the fourth of June. Em came back downstairs and grabbing her beer, sat next to me on the couch. I thanked the cop and hung up. I filled her in on what I'd just been told.

'What are you going to do for money?' I asked Em. 'I don't know. I haven't even thought about it.' 'I need a favour, can I have Davey's wheelchair? I'll pay for it.'

'I was going to sell it, it was bloody expensive.' 'No, not the electric one, yes sell that. No I want the other one, the one that you fold up to fit in the car.' 'They both fold up Charlie, but yea you can have that one.' I passed her the money. 'Shit Charlie, that's a bit OTT for a wheelchair! How much is here?' 'Ten grand. Take it. I want you to have it. It will tide you over until the insurance pays out or whatever.' 'Yes but ten thousand quid?' 'Em, if it makes you feel better then consider it a loan. Now go and put it away somewhere safe.' 'But where did you . . .' She stopped herself in mid-sentence 'I know. Don't ask.' She took the money and went upstairs. She was gone for a while so I grabbed another beer and turned on the TV. I wasn't really watching, just channel-hopping. Em came back down. She'd had a shower. She was wrapped in a towel, another one round her hair. 'Another beer?' she asked on her way through to the kitchen. 'No thanks, I've got one. I need a clear head tomorrow.' 'Why, what are you doing tomorrow? Yea I know blah blah' she said with a smile as she returned with a beer and her tin. She sat on the carpet at my feet and opening her tin she began to 'skin up'. I watched her as she made an 'L' shaped paper by sticking two rizzlas together. She then rolled a cone shaped 'spliff'. She lit it and after a couple of tokes passed it to me. I was going to say no, but thought 'sod it!' I had a few tokes and passed it back to her. I'd learned how

Black Heart

strong the stuff was last night. When she offered it to me a second time however, I did decline. 'No ta, tell you what though, you could 'ten me an oily' 'What the heck does that mean?' she asked looking puzzled.
'Roll me a fag ta. I've left my cigs in the car.' 'Yes of course but what's that got to do with whatever you just said?' As she rolled me a cig I told her the story of an old mate of mine called Jim. Or as we all called him Jim-Jimany, (as in the song Jim-Jimanie-Jim-Jimanie-Jim-Jim-Jaroo). He was a cockney. He was also a character. I'd first met him on detatchment out in the Gulf. Now cockney rhyming slang is one thing, fairly straight forward eg 'apples and pears' stairs. 'Dog and bone' phone. The trouble with Jim was he'd abbreviate the rhyme to the point of it no longer making sense. For example if he was going for a shave, he wouldn't say that he was going to dig a grave, he'd just say he was going for a dig. He did it all the time. Anyway, me and a couple of the other lads used to wind him up by inventing our own rhyming and then, like Jim, abbreviating it beyond all recognition.' 'So how does 'ten an oily' become roll me a cig?' Asked Em. 'Ah, now that was the one I was most proud of. It caught Jim out. He knew I was talking about a fag. Because an 'oily rag' is actual cockney for a fag. Ten? Well that was an abbreviation of 'ten-pin bowl.' Roll.'

'So, 'ten me an oily.' Roll me a fag!' Em looked unimpressed.
'You needed to be there. Trust me it was hilarious.' I went and got us another beer. When I returned to the lounge Em was towel drying her hair. She then unfastened the other towel and lying back seductively on the carpet she said 'See anything you like Soldier boy?' Did I?!

Afterwards, as we lay on the carpet Em asked me 'Should I Nat you a carrier?'

'What?' 'Nat King Cole you a carrier bag.Thicko!' 'Very good, for a beginner.Yes.But put me a filter in it this time ta.' When she'd finished 'natting my carrier' she said

'You do like me don't you Charlie?' I put my arm around her. 'Of course I do Em.You know I'm fond of you.It's all a bit hectic at the moment though.You've got to sort your life out. Mine's even more complicated. At the moment I'm on compassionate leave. God knows where I will be off to next, or for how long. I may not come back at all. You've already been through all that shit with Davey. Why would you want to put yourself through all that shit again? What if I got my legs blown off or . . . .?'

'Yes but you're due out soon aren't you. Surely you've done your 22 years?'

'Em. It's not that simple. I'm not in the army any more.' This time she didn't ask. She just looked at me and waited to see if I would explain.

I told her.

Chapter twenty six

Em hugged me and stroked my hair. I could feel her breath on my chest.

'Look Em, as it happens, I have been thinking of settling down. I'm getting too old for all this cloak and dagger shit. I've got a few loose ends to sort out, some officially, some not. If all goes to plan I, we, will be sorted financially.'

'Just leave now. You've got some cash; obviously, you just gave me 10 grand. My house is rented but you can sell yours. I don't know if your wife was insured but Davey was. Charlie is young enough to grow up knowing you as his dad, which you are.'

'Em. It's all very tempting. Don't you think I'd love to stop looking over my shoulder? Sleep in a nice comfy bed with a beautiful woman. Raise Charlie, maybe a few more? But we have to be realistic.How about this for a plan. I have to leave in the morning. I could be away for a day or two. I need to sort a few things out. So do you. Besides we can't go playing 'happy families' right now. Davey and Sally aren't even in the ground yet.As soon as everything's sorted we'll take it from there.'

'Yes Charlie you're right. I don't care how long it takes for us to be together, just so long as I know we will be one day.'

Black Heart

We squeezed each other tightly. She was happy. Funnily enough, I was warming to the idea too.

We lay there for several minutes. Suddenly Em stood up and grabbing my hand said

'Come Charlie, up the apples and pears, I want you to Donald Duck my Faggots out!'

'Faggots?' I said smiling 'Brains. Brains faggots. I thought you were supposed to be good at this!'

Fuck me. What had I started?

Chapter twenty seven

At 04.00 I woke up. I'd heard a noise. Lying in bed next to Em I realised it was Charlie. I needed a pee anyway so I got up. He wasn't crying, more gurgling to himself. I went for a pee. On the way back to bed I stuck my head round Charlie's bedroom door. With the light from the landing I could make him out. He was standing up in his cot. When he saw me he grinned. I went in and picked him up. I took him downstairs. I hoped Em had made up a bottle for him because I had no idea how to do it. I opened the fridge. Luckily she had made him one. I took it out and then I spotted the left-over Chinese meal. Em had been right. I was starving. I took out the various cartons and piled them next to the microwave. I knew I had to heat up the bottle, but for how long? I tried 20 seconds. I splashed a few drops on the back of my hand. That'll do I thought. I sat Charlie in his high chair and gave him the bottle. While he guzzled away at it I nuked myself some leftovers. I sat at the table near Charlie. Seeing my food he decided that it was more appetising than his bottle. He dropped his bottle to the kitchen floor and grunted at me. I got some fried rice on my fork and blowing it to cool it a little I offered it to him. He

Black Heart

grabbed a handful and proceeded to wipe it all around his face. Some of it actually went in his mouth. 15 minutes later he looked like he needed another bath. That was when Em came in. 'You boys getting to know each other are you?' 'He woke up so I thought I'd try and sort him out rather than wake you. He's had some of his bottle but I think he preferred my chinky.'
'Thanks Charlie, you go back to bed I'll sort him out from here. It was a lovely thought but there's no way he would go back to sleep for you. Looks like his nappy needs changing too. You're welcome to do it if you like!' I was half way out the kitchen by the time she'd finished that little invitation.
Even with the early hours Chinese-fest I woke at 07.00. I lay there for a while thinking about me Em and little Charlie. I was beginning to warm to the idea of us settling down togetherI'd been telling Em the truth last night when I'd said I was getting sick of looking over my shoulder. I could probably get out of my job fairly quickly on compassionate grounds. Financially we would be ok. If we moved overseas, especially somewhere like South Africa we would be laughing. We could live like royalty over there on my pension alone. Not to mention the life insurance pay outs, the proceeds of my house and contents and the cars.

What's left of the 100grand would be enough on it's own to buy a lovely place over there. Even if the £400, 000 didn't materialise. I would probably want to work anyway. I had enough contacts over there to walk into a job as a security advisor or something like that.

I slipped out of bed. Em was fast asleep. I got dressed and gave her a peck on the cheek; I was definitely getting soft in my old age. I crept out of the bedroom and left the house as quietly as possible.

Chapter twenty eight

I found the dirt track almost straight away. Not bad, I hadn't been here for years. If anything the pot-holes were even worse than I'd remembered them, forcing me to drive at about 2mph. What seemed to be miles later I came to a small car park. I got out of the car and walked to the edge of the almost sheer drop. I peered over at the vast lake. It was actually an old gravel pit. I'd fished here a few times and knew it was deep. Very deep. There was a path that led down to the pit. It went right around the water's edge. There were another two smaller pits beyond this one but they weren't accessable by car. I wouldn't be using the path. I would simply push Czeckov over the edge here, after I'd fitted him with some concrete boots.

My phone rang. My work phone. It was my boss.

'Sir?'

'Formal for you Charlie. How are you son? Coping alright?'

'Yea boss, I'm ok.'

'Have you got things sorted? Have you got anyone helping you, you know make all the arrangements and that?'

'The 'outlaws' are dealing with it. Not that there's much they can do. The cops haven't released the body yet, it's evidence and all that.'

'Quite, quite.Listen Charlie, I know you're on leave but the thing is we could do with your report on your last 'trip'. Have you had chance to write it up yet?'

'Yea boss, I did it on the flight home.'

'Ok good. I'll send a driver over to your digs to pick it up.'

'I'm not actually there boss; I went out for a drive, clear my head. I can be back there in about an hour.'

'Good man Charlie. Take care, and ring me if you need anything.' He hung up.

Fuck it. Mind you I'd seen all I needed to see here. It was just a balls-ache having to go back to my digs. I needed to be going in the opposite direction. Never mind I should be ok for time. I just hoped the driver wasn't late.

I got back in the hire car and drove to Wooton Bassett.

Chapter twenty nine

As I drove into London My thoughts turned from what lay ahead. I thought about John Kenny. The lucky bastard had slipped from second to forth on my list. Maybe even fifth if I had to take out Checkov's bodyguard. Then I thought about Dimitri, the sly bastard. He'd sneaked that little detail under the radar. He'd also been very vague about who was financing the hit on Checkov. Suddenly my mind snapped back to the job in hand. Just ahead on the pavement was what I'd been looking for. A beggar. I pulled up alongside the homeless guy. He was sitting on the pavement with his back to an office block. He was wrapped in a blanket, a trilby style hat at his feet. I powered down the passenger side window and shouted across to him 'Do you want to earn yourself a ton?' 'I'm not gay.' He replied. 'Neither am I, 10 minutes work100 quid, yes or no?' A slight hesitation then he got to his feet. 'In the back, bring the hat and blanket with you.' As if he would leave any of his possessions behind! Having said that, I'd read about some of these beggars that were making a fortune, especially out of tourists. They may look like they haven't got a pot to piss in, but in reality they live in a better house than me. 'So what's the plan man?' Said the homeless as he approached the car.

'Simple.' I said. 'We walk into a hotel'
'Whoa!' he interrupted 'I told you I'm not a rent-boy.' 'Yes I know' I said waving a £50 note. 'You get this now. We walk into a hotel and get in the lift. You then walk out with another one of these.' 'And that's all I have to do?' 'That's all, except you will need to be in a wheelchair.' 'As long as you don't go touching me up that's fine by me.' He got in the back seat and leaned forward to grab the note from my hand. A few minutes later I pulled up outside the Barbican Hotel. I popped the boot and got out of the hire car. As the doorman approached I passed him my holdall I took out the wheelchair, unfolded it and went to the rear passenger door. The beggar got into it. To be fair he actually played the part and made it look like a struggle. I stuck his hat on his head, draped his blanket round him and pushed him towards the entrance. I took my holdall from the doorman and sat it on the beggar's knees. (If only he knew what he was holding)? I gave the doorman my car keys and a £20 note. 'Mr Chekovski, I have a reservation. Can you get someone to park my car? Tell them to make sure I can get to it easily, as I may need to go out later.' He tipped his hat 'Certainly Sir.'
'Not a word. Pretend to be asleep.' I said to the beggar as I wheeled him to the reception desk.

'Mr Czeckovski, I have a reservation.' I said to the smiling receptionist. As she typed my name I only had to lean forward slightly on the desk to see what I was looking for. Above my name on the screen was what I was looking for. Czeckov. Room 301. Result.

'Oh that's strange. You're Mr Czeckovski and we have a Mr Czeckov staying too.' Said the girl. This could be easier than I'd planned.

'Yes I know'. I said. 'He's a friend of mine.'

'Oh did you want to be next to him? Only that could be tricky as you're in a special facility room and I can't really move Mr Czeckov as he's already booked in.'

'No that's fine. Tell me though; has Mr Czeckov booked a table for dinner in the restaurant?'

'One second sir. Yes he has. Table for four at 7.30.'

'Ok that's fine. He's booked for us as well.'

'Could you fill in this registration form please sir? And do you have a credit card?'

'I will be paying cash.' I told her.

'Yes sir but I still need to take your card details.'

'Oh I see.' I said handing her the card from my top pocket. 'Is that in case I run up a huge phone bill or watch loads of porn on TV and leave without paying?' She blushed.

'Only joking, I know you're just doing your job.' She finished taking my card details and passed it back to me, along with my key card.

'Room 104 sir. Do you require any help with, er?'

'My son. No thanks, we're fine.'

The lift door slid open on the first floor. I stepped out and held the door open with the wheelchair. The lad stood up. I told him to put the holdall in the chair along with the hat and blanket. He was about to protest until I passed him 2 fifties. I pressed 7 on the control panel with my elbow. 'Go up in the lift then come back down to reception and off you go'

'Cheers.' He said as I removed the wheelchair and watched the lift door close.

Chapter thirty

I inserted the key card into the slot and turned the handle. I pushed the wheelchair into the room and before closing the door I wiped the handle on my t-shirt. I checked my watch.It was 7.00pm. This would be tight. Czeckov could be leaving his room at any time to have a drink at the bar before dinner. I had to get him now. I unzipped the holdall, took out a pair of latex gloves and pulled them on. I picked up the Glock and fitted the silencer. I removed the magazine, checked it and re-inserted it. I cocked the weapon and applying the safety, tucked it in my jeans at the small of my back I re-zipped the holdall, covered it with the blanket and opening the door I pushed the wheelchair along the corridor to the lift.

I pushed the button to call the lift.It was coming down.Good.Less chance of anyone being in it. Unless. Oh shit, they couldn't be. As the door slid open, there they stood, Czeckov and his minder. Shit. Five minutes earlier and I would've got them in their room. I pressed 3. Would it go back up? No damn it, the lift began to descend.

The bodyguard had seen my gloved hand and was obviously suspicious. He began to reach inside his jacket. I pulled the Glock and pushed it to his forehead. The lift reached the ground floor. The doors slid open.

I stood with my back to the open lift door. I had the Glock pressed into the bodyguards groin; it wouldn't be visible from behind. After what seemed an eternity the doors slid shut and we began to ascend. I reached inside the bodyguard's jacket and removed his 9mm; I tucked it in my waistband. I picked up the blanket and draped it over my arm to conceal the Glock. I put on the hat and lifting my holdall out of the wheelchair I told the minder to sit. I dumped the holdall on his lap.

'Keep your hands where I can see them Sergey.' I told him. The lift doors opened. I stepped back and glanced left and right.

'Ok Czeckov, push your man to your room.'

'Whoever you are, you will regret this.' He said.

'Cut the chat and push.' I told him. As soon as we were inside the room I gave the bodyguard the good news. Double-tap to the back of the head. He slumped forward in the wheelchair. I pushed him out onto the floor. Simples!

'Sit.' I said to Czeckov jesturing toward the wheelchair.

'You won't get away with . . .' I silenced him mid-complaint with a blow to the back of the head with the butt of the Glock.

I unzipped my holdall and took out the hyperdermic needle. I removed the shield and injected the colourless liquid into a vein in his neck.

I didn't need him waking up and kicking off. Oh I was going to shoot him.But not here.

I didn't want to wheel him through reception pissing blood everywhere. I placed the hat on his head and draped the blanket across his legs. I re-zipped my holdall and putting it on his lap, wheeled him out the door, down the hall to the lift. When it arrived I pressed 'G' then removed my gloves and stuck them in my pocket.

At reception I saw there had been a shift change as a pretty black girl gave me a smile as I approached. 'Mr Czechovski, room 104, could I have my car keys please?'

'Certainly sir, I'll get them for you.' As she looked for my keys I glanced across to the bar. There were two men in suits stood at the bar. I thought I recognised one of them.

'Here you are sir, your keys. Your car is in bay 7. You can take the lift to the basement, or I can have it brought around to the front door for you.'

'That won't be necessary thank you I will take the lift.'

As the lift doors were closing I noticed one of the 'suits' making his way towards reception.

To put a call up to Czeckov's room maybe? I'd definitely seen him before, but couldn't remember where.

The lift began to descend to the basement.

That had been close.Fucking close.

Chapter thirty one

I found the hire car reasonably easily. I was going to dump Czeckov in the boot. However looking around the car park I noticed 'Big brother' was on my case. There were CCTV cameras all over the place. I went through the motions of helping him into the back seat and attatching his seat belt. I then collapsed the wheelchair and put it in the boot. That was a bit of a squeeze considering all of the goodies I'd bought the previous day. I drove off, making my way through remarkably light traffic. I made such good progress that I almost missed my turning onto the M25. Even the world's largest car park was without the usual tailbacks. Within 45 minutes I was on the A40 heading to Oxford. I stuck to 75mph I didn't need the 'old bill' pulling me for speeding, not with old Boris in the back seat.

As I worked my way around the ring roads of Oxford I had to slow down. I was now coming in the opposite direction than earlier in the day, it was also dark. Yep, sure enough I'd missed the turning for the dirt track. At the first opportunity I did a u-turn. Once on the track I turned the car lights off. It was a moon-lit night and I was travelling all of 2mph so it wasn't a problem to see where I was going. Good job I did turn the lights off, because it soon became evident that I was not alone. Before I even got to

the car park I could see lights. I stopped and turned the engine off. I jogged along the grass at the side of the dirt road, it would be less noisy. Just before the car park I had a perfect view down towards the gravel pit. Fuck! There were 5 'Bivies' set up along the bank. A group of young guys were sat around a fire drinking cans of beer as they waited for a 'beep' from their optomics. Carp fishing at this time of year, they must be mad! Not as mad as me, I was fucking livid!
Time for plan 'B.' Except I didn't have one. As I walked back to the car I lit a cigarette. I checked my watch 9.35pm. I phoned Em.
'Change of plan. Can I come round yours?'
'You're welcome to 'come' round mine any time you like Charlie!'
'Tart! I'll be half an hour or so, depending on the traffic.'
'Are you hungry, do you want anything to eat?'
Now she'd mentioned it, it suddenly occurred to me that I'd had nothing to eat since my midnight-supper with little Charlie.
'No don't go messing around at this time of night; I'll pick something up on the way to yours. Do you want anything?'
'Do I really need to answer that big boy? Joking.No I'll just pinch a bit of whatever you get. See you soon.'

Chapter thirty two

When I got back to the car there was no choice other than to reverse back the way I'd just come. Half way back to the main road I passed a reasonable looking piece of ground on my right, so drove into it and did a three-point-turn. A couple of hundred metres from the main road I stopped the car. The makings of 'Plan B' were forming in my head. I popped the boot and dumped the bags of sand, cement and buckets in the bushes. Mr 'C' wouldn't be 'sleeping with the fishes' tonight. I couldn't shoot him either, considering he would be spending at least one night in the boot of my hire car. I took one of the tarpaulin sheets from the boot and spread it on the ground. I then got him out of the back of the car and laid him on it.

 I took the shovel from the boot and placed it across his throat. Standing, legs astride either side of his head, I jumped on the handle, snapping his neck, crushing his larynx and basically snuffing him out without any blood-flow. I placed the Glock and the bodyguard's 9mm on top of him before wrapping up the tarp' with gaffa-tape. I lifted him into the boot. I ignored the bag full of crisps and chocky that was screaming for my attention, as I'd already set my heart on fish, chips and mushy peas.

Just when I thought nothing else could go wrong today I pulled up outside the 'chippy' near Em's, only to find it was closed. Oh well, at least the Indian take-away was open.
I didn't know if Em liked spicey food so I ordered a vindaloo and a korma, popadoms chutney and naan. I felt sure there'd be something she'd eat. If not I'd have it!
When I tapped quietly on the door of Em's house at 10.15 she answered it in a cellotape nightie. Well it wasn't cellotape but it was just as see-through. As I shut the door behind me she said 'Apples.'
'You've lost me there girl.' I said.
'Remember what we were talking about last night? The abbreviating rhyming slang and all that? I said to you 'Up the apples and pears etc'so I'm seriously abbreviating now 'Apples!'
I could see my curry going cold!

Chapter thirty three

The next morning I was awakened by my phone buzzing. I'd received a text message. I looked at my watch, frigging 3am. The text read 'Peregrine'. I got out of bed and went downstairs. I text back 'Falcon'. A few moments later my phone rang. It was of course Dimitri.

'Hi Charlie. I just saw the news. Czeckov is missing. Was that you or is it just a coincidence?'

'It was me and the clock's ticking. Don't make me chase you for my money.'

'Ok buddy. Shit I just thought, it's 3am there right?'

'Yes it is. Now fuck off and let me go back to sleep.'

There was actually no chance of me doing that, I was now wide awake. I switched on the TV.

Turning the volume right down, I flicked through the news channels. As Dimitri was in the States I guessed he must've been watching CNN or possibly Sky News. The story was covered on both. There wasn't actually that much of a story. A man had been found shot dead in his hotel room. His colleague, a wealthy Russian businessman was missing. The body of the dead man, who had not yet been named, had been discovered by hotel staff.

They had been asked to check on the whereabouts of the two men when they'd failed to show up for dinner.

I switched the TV off and tip-toed back upstairs and got dressed. Grabbing Monty I quietly left the house and drove back to the B&B.

I had several things to do but it was still too early. Changing into my trackies and trainers I went for a jog. Taking my now familiar route, I payed particular attention as I went through the graveyard. I didn't see what I was looking for, so headed back to my digs for a 'Full English.' Elsie, the landlady did a fine fry-up.

After breakfast and a shower I tried phoning the car-hire company. It was just after 08 00.

My call was answered. I made up some excuse about not liking my hire car and arranged to swap it for a different model. They'd offered to bring the replacement car to me to swap them over.

'Yeah sure, excuse the dead body in the boot!' No, I'd arranged to bring the car to them in about an hour.

I drove to the dirt track behind John Kenny's house. In the second of the abandoned farm buildings was a stack of wooden pallets. Popping the boot I dragged Czeckov's body behind them. Not ideal but I'd only be leaving him here for an hour or so.

Black Heart

I drove to the car-hire firm to swap vehicles, stopping on the way to top up the fuel, as per my contract. Checks done, paperwork completed and Monty swapped from one boot to another, I was back at the barn and loading Czeckov into the boot of my replacement hire car in next to no time.

Chapter thirty four

My phone rang. My private phone, not the work phone. It was Em.
'Hi Em, one sec I'm driving.' I pulled into the side of the road.
'What's up?'
'Well I don't know if I'm very happy with you Charlie Higgins! You turn up and ravish me then disappear like a thief in the night! Only kidding. You're welcome to come and ravish me any time you like. I was just ringing to find out if you're planning on coming over tonight.'
'No Em I can't tonight. Tomorrow maybe. I'll ring you.'
'Ok' she said. She didn't sound too happy.
'Cheer up. Do what you girls do best, get some retail therapy!'
'I might just do that, that wad of cash you gave me is burning a hole in my bedroom drawer. I think I might treat myself to some sexy new underwear. That might get you round here sooner.'
'You bet it will. I'll look forward to it. You can put on an X-rated fashion show for me if you like.'
'I might just do that. See you tomorrow then?'
'I'll try, but no promises. Have fun shopping.' I hung up and pulled back out into the traffic. I had some shopping of my own to do.

Black Heart

At the DIY store I got everything on my mental list. A shovel, a roll of heavy-duty bin liners and some rope. Loading my purchases into the hire car I drove back to the B&B
I'd forgotten to buy today's newspaper so I picked up the unfinished crossword from the other day. Doing a crossword on this bed was like counting sheep. When I woke up it was 8.15pm.
After a quick wash and shave to wake me up I decided to go into town to get a bite to eat, and have a couple of pints. It was a fairly pleasant evening so I decided to walk rather than drive. I got a wet-weather jacket out of the car, just in case the weather forecast I'd heard on the car radio turned out to be correct. Well even weather forecasters got it right sometimes.

Chapter thirty five

After a steady walk to Wooton Bassett I arrived at 'The Happy Kebab'just before 9.00pm.
I ordered my meal and stood outside and had a fag whilst it was being prepared. Looked like the forecasters got it right, it started to pee it down with rain. I was glad I'd brought my jacket. I stubbed out my cig and went back inside, sitting at my usual table in the window. By 9.30 I'd finished my meal but took my time drinking my drink as I wanted to see if Kenny would be true to form. Sure enough, at 9.40pm he pulled into the car park opposite me. He got out and strut-wobbled (well he was trying to strut but it looked more like a wobble to me) towards the pub. Interesting, he hadn't locked his truck. Just as I had that thought, his hazards flashed, and I clearly heard the central-locking.Figures.I might've known he would be one of those 'look how far I can be from my car and still lock it' poser types.Shame.It would make my life easier if he didn't lock his truck.
With Kenny in the Lion I decided against drinking in there. Instead I walked the 50 or so yards down the road and had a few pints at the Crown.

Chapter thirty six

The next few days were pretty 'same same'. I'd jogged both mornings. Usual route, still no joy in the cemetery. I'd spent hours on the phone to estate agents. The cops had finally given me permission to go to my own house. I got there about an hour before the first guy came round to value the place. Just as well really as I had some tidying up to do! The bedroom was exactly as I'd last seen it. Minus a corpse. The bedclothes wine glasses and bottles had gone too. Evidence, no doubt. I got some linen from the airing cupboard and made the bed. Downstairs I washed the dishes. Something in the pedal-bin didn't smell too fresh so I emptied it. I had a quick tidy round and then sprayed air-freshener and furniture polish everywhere. I picked up a pile of mail and sorted through it. Dropping the junk in the bin I put the rest in my pocket to look at later. The first couple of valuers turned up almost at the same time. The third was late, so while waiting I took the opportunity to get a few more pairs of socks and bits and pieces and loaded them in the car. Once all the valuers had been and gone I locked up and left.

I'd also kept an eye on Kenny.I could've set my watch by him. I'd spoken to Em several times on the phone. In our last conversation just before I went to bed she'd made me promise to come and see her the next day.

'Ok, ok I'll see you tomorrow 6pm I promise.'

Chapter thirty seven

The next morning, after my usual jog, Id just got out of the shower and could hear my phone ringing. I got to it just before my answer-phone kicked in.

'Mr Higgins?' It was the DI.

'DI Jenkins. I have some rather good news for you. About one hour ago Gross was found hanging in his cell. We're not sure yet but it would appear to be a suicide.'

'That should save us tax-payers some money. Thanks for letting me know. Have you told the wife's parents yet?'

'That will be my next call sir.'

'Ok thanks again, bye'.

I went downstairs for one of Elsie's fry-ups. I had a few more mundane things to sort out before heading over to Em's. I found myself looking forward to that. I was definitely going soft.

As I got in the hire car I had a sniff. Nothing. I thanked God it wasn't the height of summer. Czeckov would be ponging like hell by now. This was the 4th day he'd been in my boot. I might have to come up with a plan 'C' for our Mr 'C'.

After a boring day at the bank, building society and estate agents I was glad to be on my way to Em's. As I said I was looking forward to it. She'd promised me a surprise, and I don't think she was talking about dinner.

I was literally about 5mins from her house when my phone rang. It was her. I ignored it I would be there soon. It rang out but immediately rang again. Maybe she wanted me to pick some milk up or something? I pulled the car over. I'd got a body in the boot for God's sake. I answered.

'Charlie, there are two men here with guns they . . . .' A man's voice came on the phone.

'Charlie you have a friend of mine. Is he well? I hope so. Your friend and her son are also well. At the moment they are well' He was foreign.Russian. 'You sound like you are in a vehicle, this is good. We would like for you to come here. We will be expecting you in (pause-obviously to ask Em how long it should take me) One hour and twenty minutes.'

'Yes I will be there.If you harm . . . .' the line went dead.

Chapter thirty eight

Ok I had the element of surprise on my side. They weren't expecting me for quite some time but I was literally just around the corner. I did have one problem though, a weapon. Sure I had my 9mm Browning behind me in my holdall. I also had Davey's, although that wasn't loaded. The thing was, I needed a weapon with a silencer. The Glock was wrapped in a tarp, along with Czeckov's corpse, in the boot of my car. I pulled to the side of the road and got busy with a pen-knife, hacking at the gaffa-tape. Actually it could've been worse, if plan 'A' had worked out, the Glock would've been in one of Czeckovs concrete boots, at the bottom of a gravel pit. I eventually managed to retrieve the gun, and having checked, cocked and applying the safety, stuffed it in my waistband. I drove to within 50mtrs of Em's house. If, as I now feared, they had somehow managed to trace my last hire car, I should be fine. This was a different colour and model. Besides they wouldn't be expecting me for ages yet. I jogged as quickly as possible, using the hedge rows for cover. It was dark and the street lighting was pretty crap. At the end of Em's driveway I stopped and peered around the hedge. There was a black

Mercedes parked nose-in, the boot open and a huge guy was leaning in looking for something. I glanced up and down the street.All clear.In three strides I was right behind him. Pop pop. Double tap to the back of the head.As he collapsed forward I helped him on his way into the boot. I shut the boot lid, as I did the registration plate came into view. Interesting, Diplomatic Plates.

Em had said two men. Did that mean one down one to go? Or had two men entered the house and this was a third? Hopefully not. Even with the element of surprise, one more was definitely better than two more.

Keeping to the shadows I made my way along the side of the house, over the low gate, to the back of the property. The curtains were drawn in the lounge but I could see the lights were on in there. The kitchen light was also on and through the window I could see Em holding a crying Charlie, doing the hip thing, making a bottle. No sign of the other Russian/s. I tried the door. It was locked. I tapped gently on the window and held my face close so that she would see it was me.I jestured with my finger to my lips for her to be quiet. I then pointed to the door and mimed unlocking it. She did. I opened it and grabbing her arm, pulled her and Charlie outside. I led them quickly down the garden.

'How many in there Em?' 'One, the other guy went out to the car for something.'

'Yeah we met. Stay low in these shadows, it won't be long before the other one thinks you've done a runner and comes out looking for you.'

I moved quickly over to the house and crouched low in the shadows near the open back door. Seconds later the Russian stepped out, a PPK in his outstretched hands. He turned in my direction but before he could adjust his aim downwards at me, I had emptied the mag into his chest. He fell like a ton of bricks. I picked up his weapon and stuck it in my belt.

Chapter thirty nine

Five minutes later Em sat in the kitchen feeding Charlie his bottle, at the same time drinking the strong black coffee that I'd made for her. I was stood just outside the back door smoking a cig and sipping on a 'wobbly'.

'I take it those two were one of the 'loose ends' you spoke about the other night?'

'Fraid so.' I said. 'I'm sorry Em, I had no idea they would turn up here. At the moment I'm not sure how they did. I'm just glad you and Charlie are ok. We can't stay here. As soon as Charlie's finished his bottle you need to go and pack some things. I'll clean up out here. Ok?' She nodded. Stubbing out my cig and finishing my beer I set to work. I pulled a tarpaulin sheet from a patio set it was covering and wrapped 'Boris' in it. I dragged him over to the gate. I then turned on the garden hose and using a broom scrubbed away at the pool of blood that had formed where he'd lain. The paving slabs looked as good as new. Granted they wouldn't stand up to close scrutiny from a 'scenes of crime team', but why would they even be looking? Once I'd got rid of these two jokers and their vehicle there would be no reason for the police to link them to this address.

Black Heart

In truth it wasn't the police I was worried about.
The reason we were getting 'the flock out of here' was because, if whoever sent these two heavies round here didn't hear from them, you could bet they would be sending in the cavalry.
Checking there was nobody in the street I dragged the dead gunman to the Mercedes and lay him on the back seat. I had a slight panic when I couldn't locate the keys. Eventually though I popped the boot and found them in the other dead Russian's pocket. I locked the car and went back around the house and in through the kitchen door. Charlie was in his play-pen as his mum was busy packing all the 'gubbins' associated with toddlers. When she'd finished I took her case and bags out to my hire car, piling them on top of Czeckov. It was a tight squeeze so some of her kit had to go on the floor in the back of the car. With Em's help we fitted Charlie's car-seat in the back. A quick check of the house to make sure everything was secure etc. and we were off.
'Follow me.' I said getting into the Merc' and reversed out of the driveway. I checked in the mirror that Em was following in my car and headed for the A40. I had no idea where I was going. I was just getting some distance between us and the house. Think Charlie, think.

Chapter forty

About 20minutes into the journey there was a sudden noise behind me. Shit, that made me jump! It was a phone ringing. It rang for a while and then fell silent. I then heard a more muffled ring tone eminating from the boot. Whoever was at the other end of the phones now knew that something was wrong. It wouldn't be long before re-inforcements would be on their way to Em's house, or . . . Shit! The penny dropped. That was how they'd turned up at Em's.

I could see a lay-by up ahead. I indicated and saw in my mirror that Em had also. We both pulled in. A few hundred metres later we stopped. It was one of those massive lay-bys that goes round in a horse-shoe and then re-joins the carriageway. It was deserted. Later in the night it would probably be full of HGV's, their drivers catching 40 winks. Just up ahead was an old coach that had been converted into a café. It was closed.

I got out and opened the back door. Rooting through the Russian's pocket I located the phone. I popped the boot and did the same with the other guy. Again a phone, and also a 9mm.

Black Heart

I disconnected the batteries on both phones.I walked to Em and she powered down the window. 'What's wrong Charlie?'
'Don't worry, stay in the car out of the cold. Just pop the boot for me please, Em.'
There was no need for her to know there was also a body in the boot of the car she was driving! It took a while to get to Czeckov's phone. I had to unload Em's luggage and then bloody unwrap him again. His phone was off and I couldn't turn it on. The battery was dead. That confirmed my suspicions. I'd bet good money that it had died the night Id stayed at Em's with Czeckovs body in the boot.Careless Charlie.Fucking careless.
I took the battery off anyway. I dumped all three phones in the boot and, reloading all of the luggage, shut the lid. I got in the front passenger seat next to Em to explain the unscheduled stop.
'Have you seen the 'find my phone App' that you can get for smart phones now?' I asked her.' 'Yes I know what you mean.'
'Well the security services have had that technology for years, so have the Russians. That's how your visitors found us. Take the battery off your phone and do these aswell.'I said passing her both my phones. 'Stay in the car and keep the engine running. Watch for my signal.' I got out and walked to the Merc'.

110

Here was as good as anywhere to torch it. There was a copse of trees between us and the main road. The car would be well alight before it was noticed by any passing traffic. The other bonus was that this was the exact location where the Russians' phones had stopped transmitting. Their friends would turn up here, to a dead-end.Literally.

Chapter forty one

Unfortunately the Merc' was a diesel. It would burn, but you couldn't just stick a burning rag in the fuel tank as you could with a petrol-engined car. Looking around my eyes settled on the café. I trotted over and checked it out. It looked promising. There were a coulple of large gas cylinders chained up outside the coach. I forced the lock on the coach door. Inside I found a catering-sized 5 gallon tub of cooking oil. I took the oil outside along with a roll of blue paper towel. Picking the lock on the padlock I undid the chain and dragged one of the gas bottles over to the Merc'. I opened the back door and lay it on the floor. I then opened the window slightly and stuffed the end of the blue paper towel through. I walked back towards the café unrolling the blue paper behind me. I opened the tub of oil and as I slowly made my way back to the car I dribbled it all over the kitchen towel. At the car I emptied the oil all over the interior. I opened the valve on the gas bottle and then closed the car door. I waved at Em and motioned her to come. She pulled up alongside me. 'Drive past me and stop about 50 metres past that coach. Keep the engine running. It could get a little 'dramatic' in a minute.' As soon as she pulled away I lit my makeshift fuse and ran like hell behind her. When she stopped I jumped in and told her to 'Go, Go. Go!'

Kerboom! It sounded like a bomb going off. As we fed into the traffic on the A40 there was a second smaller explosion, the fuel tank presumably.

About an hour later, as we approached London I saw a signpost for a Travel-lodge. I told Em to turn in.

We checked in, and while Em took Charlie up to the family room we'd booked I went out to the car to get our luggage. Looking at Czeckov's body I couldn't help wishing I'd put him in the Merc' before I'd torched it. It would've cost me 400grand but at least I'd have been rid of him.And the people that were looking for him.

I took the luggage to the room. 'Back soon, just gonna find an all-night garage or something and get us some provisions.' I gave her a quick hug. 'You ok?'

'Charlie, this may have been a normal day at the office for you but I'm shattered, mentally and physically.'

'Have a hot bath or something, sort the laddo out and I'll be back asap.' I kissed her and left the room. At reception I got directions to a 24hr Tesco's that was only a few miles away.

Chapter forty two

At the store I quickly filled a basket with snacks. Sausage rolls, pork pies crisps etc. not forgetting a couple of bottles of wine. I also picked up a few 'Vodaphone' SIM cards and at the till I got two £10 pay-as-you-go credits.
Back at the Travel-lodge I tapped on our room door and Em let me in.
Little Charlie was sat on the double bed watching cartoons. His little eyes lit up when I tipped a couple of carrier bags full of junk food onto the bed. We all had a pic-nic, scoffing crisps, sausage rolls and sarnies. There were crumbs everywhere, so much so that we had to gather up the duvet and take it into the bathroom to shake it out in the bath. While Em sorted Charlie out, I took a shower, disposing of the debris from our pic-nic down the plug hole with my feet. By the time I'd showered Charlie was dead to the world in the single bed. Em went for a shower and I poured us some wine, in coffee cups! While Em was in the bathroom I sorted out our phones, fitting new SIM's and loading the credit. I stuck my old SIM in my wallet. I had a 'gizzmo' that would transfer all my data to my new SIM. But I didn't have it with me.

I rang Em's phone from mine and vice-versa, hence leaving missed calls with our new numbers on each phone, which I duly filed.Hey, if you're 'down with the kids' that's the way they do it these days. Heaven forbid they write their number down.On paper, with a pen.

When Em came out of the shower, wrapped in a towel she sat next to me on the bed. I gave her her phone and told her she needed to text all the important people her new number. 'You have got their numbers on your phone memory, I hope.'

'Yes I always save to phone and SIM.'

'Lucky, you'd have been stuffed otherwise!' I had been taught to always save to both. I often used a spare SIM if I wanted to make a call and not leave my number and it still allowed you to access your contacts (eg when I'd phoned Gross.) 'Witholding' your number didn't work. It could still be traced back to you.

Big Brother.

We had a few more 'glasses' of wine. Em was looking a little less stressed as the alcohol took effect.

I put my arm around her and re-assured her that everything would be fine.

She just couldn't go back home for a while.

Chapter forty three

As we lay in bed Em suddenly turned on her bedside light.
'Charlie. Who were those men and why did they come to my house?'
'You don't want to know.'
'That's just it Charlie, I do. Today, me and Charlie got dragged into your world. I think you owe me an explanation. I'm not asking you to break the official secrets act. Mind you something tells me that this wasn't 'official'. 'Not entirely.'
'See Charlie, there you go again, talking in riddles. Black or white Charlie.'
'There lies the problem Em. It never is black or white. More like grey.
Ok. I was asked to kill a man. It's what I do. He wasn't a very nice man. In fact he was a very bad man. Now this is where we go from black and white to grey. The bad man is not the issue. Who asked me to kill him is the issue. If my boss had asked me to kill him I would've received nothing except maybe some 'smartie points', oh and the pittance they call my salary. Someone else asked me and he was willing to pay me a lot of money.
Now here's the thing. The man is dead. My client is happy. My boss won't be unhappy.

Officially of course he would have to be if he knew who'd done it. Ironically it could've been the other way round. I could've been asked 'officially' to kill the man. When I did, my boss would've been happy. The man who'd almost spent a lot of money to have him killed woud've been delighted. Either way, we still would've had a visit from 'the chuckle brothers.' Actually that last statement wasn't strictly true. I'd cocked up. I decided to come clean.

'I inadvertently led those two to your house. The night I killed Czeckov, that was his name, I'd intended to dispose of his body in a lake. Unfortunately, there were fishermen there, so I couldn't. I came and spent the night at yours. He, or rather his phone, spent the night in the boot of my hire car, parked on your driveway. Some time during the night the battery on his phone went dead. That's why they came to your house. It was the last place they'd received a signal from his phone.'

'They can be that accurate?' 'Yep, I'm afraid so. I'm sorry I dragged you into my world Em. Truly I am. If you and Charlie want to leave, I wouldn't blame you. All I can say is that I don't want that. I want us to be together. A family.'

'Yes Charlie. I want that too.' We kissed each other goodnight.

Chapter forty four

I woke at 07.00. Em and Charlie were still asleep. I rinsed the wine stains from the cups and made coffee. I took the cups over to the bed. Em woke up when I sat on the edge of the bed. She sat up and took the cup of coffee from me. She glanced across at little Charlie.
'Do you want to go down for breakfast?' I asked.
'Little Charlie is still asleep. We need to take advantage of that. I fancy 'sausage' for my breakfast!'
'You little slut!' I said, getting back in bed with her.
After we'd showered and Em had got little Charlie ready, we went down to the dining room. Over breakfast we discussed what we were going to do next.
'The best thing you can do is take Charlie to your mum and dad's for a few days. Would they be up for that?'
'Are you kidding? Mum would jump at the chance.'
'Ok that's settled then. I've got some loose ends to tie up. That should only take a few days.' Em raised an eyebrow.
'Nothing 'dodgy.'House sale, funeral arrangements etc. Have your parents sorted out Davey's funeral yet?'I asked, changing the subject. I did have a few 'dodgy' things to sort out. I had a corpse to get rid of for a start.

Then there was the matter of John Kenny. He just kept slipping down the list! If I included Gross' suicide he was now at number eight.

'I'll phone her now, ask if we can stay and find out about the funeral.' While Em phoned her mum I went out to reception to organise a hire car for her. We would be going our separate ways for a couple of days so it made more sense for her to have her own vehicle.

'Sorted?' I asked when I got back to the table.

'Yes. Mum's delighted. I'm going to leave Charlie with dad, and me and mum are going shopping.'

'Good. Buy some nice shorts and bikinis. When everything's sorted we're out of here.'

'Where?'

'I was thinking South Africa.' I said.

'Sounds great to me, I can't wait.' Leaving Em spooning soggy weetabix into Charlie I went up to the room and collected our luggage. I loaded my kit into my car. I left their stuff at reception. Her hire car should be here very soon. In fact here it was now. I'd signed for the car, helped the driver fit Charlie's car seat and loaded her kit just in time. Em and Charlie came out.

Her face was a picture as she was handed the keys to the bright blue Renault cabriolet.

I kissed them goodbye and got into my crappy hire car.

'Be careful Charlie.'

'I will. Stop worrying. I'll phone you later.' I'd made a mistake. I wasn't planning on making any more.

Chapter forty five

Back at the B&B I made a few phone calls to find out what had been happening back on planet earth. When I eventually got round to ringing the mother-in-law Jeees. I was half expecting some ear-ache. I got it with trumps.

'We've been trying to get hold of you nag nag nag . . . .'

'Yes I'm sorry Liz. I lost my phone with all my contact numbers on and it's taken me ages to . . .'

'Anyway,' she cut me off 'Seeing as that evil bastard topped himself, the cops have finally released poor Sally's body, so she can be laid to rest. You should've been organising all this, but as you were busy being the invisible man, me and Ronald have made all the arrangements. And notified everybody. And sorted out food and drinks. And flowers, blah blah.' Every now and then, as she paused for breath I'd managed to get a 'Thank you' or a 'Good' into the conversation. Anyway the bottom line seemed to be that, no thanks to me, she had sorted the whole thing. Starting with the church service at 10.00 am tomorrow morning and the burial at 11.15.

'We will be doing drinks and sandwiches at our house after the burial blah blah. You could at least thank me.' That was me told.

'Sorry Liz, I thought I had. Yes thanks a lot.' God I was going to miss her. Not. No wonder comedians make a living out of mother-in-law sketches. Of course I never had been good enough for their 'little princess'. Still, after the funeral I doubted that I'd ever see them again.

'Thanks again Liz. I couldn't have coped without you and Ron. I'll see you at the church in the morning.' I hung up before she could say anything. She hated me referring to her huband as 'Ron.' 'It's RonALD.' She would say.

I then killed an hour or so checking things with the estate agents to see how things were progressing with the sale of the house. I also plugged in my 'gizzmo' and downloaded all my apps etc to my phone. Checking through my contacts I found names of people that I didn't even know who they were. I deleted them. I toyed with the idea of driving into Swindon to buy a new suit. I had a funeral tomorrow and another one within a day or two. I decided against it. Sod it. I had a suit that would be fine. I wasn't planning on wearing a suit again after this week. I was planning on living in shorts and t-shirts for the foreseeable. Instead, I picked up today's edition of the 'I' that I'd picked up on my way back. I did my usual trick. I lay on the bed and started to do the crossword.

When I woke up it was 5.00pm. It was already dark. I changed into my running kit. I set off on my now familiar circuit.

Cutting through the cemetery I finally saw what I'd been looking for all week. Not one but three of them. Two side by side and another, a bit further away, behind some trees. That one looked the best. 'Like buses.' That's what my old man would've said. 'You can't bloody get one, then three come along all at once!' I continued my run back to the B&B. After a quick shower I drove to my house. I got my dark suit from my wardrobe, along with a white shirt and a black tie. Downstairs I got the can of WD40 from the cupboard under the sink. I hung my suit on the hanger above the back door in the hire car and drove to Wooton Bassett to get something to eat. The 'Bell' had a good reputation for food, especially the steak. I loved steak and really fancied one. I'd been living on junk-food recently, and today I'd not eaten since breakfast at the Travel lodge.

Black Heart

I had a pint at the bar and asked to see the menu. Pointless really, I'd already decided on the 32oz steak with all the trimmings. I gave the barmaid my order. 'Pink no blood.' being my answer to the inevitable question whenever you order a steak. As I finished my beer a waitress came through to the bar to show me to my table. I ordered a glass of house red and it arrived along with half a cow. It was a struggle but I finished the steak. I left half of the chips though. I paid my bill and left. 9.15pm Too early to go to the cemetery, but I did have something else to take care of.
I drove to the dirt track near John Kenny's house.

Chapter forty six

Behind the derelict buildings was an ideal place to hide my ever-increasing arsenal. I parked in one of the empty barns. I put on a pair of latex gloves then ripped a bin liner from the roll and layed it on the ground. I wiped down all the weapons and layed them out on it. Davey's 9mm Browning, Sergey's Luger, the chuckle brothers two PPK's and finally the Glock. I gave them a good spray with the WD40 and then turned the bin liner inside out and tied a knot in it. I placed it into another bin bag. Before knotting it I dropped a 25k bundle of cash in. I dug a 3ft hole and buried the life-sentence-worth of evidence. Placing a few rocks on top I just hoped there were no amateur metal-detector types in the area.

Originally I'd planned on burying the cell-phones aswell. I'd decided against that because they may hold useful information that may pre-warn me about who I was trying to avoid. I had no doubt that all the info would be in Russian. I didn't speak Russian. But I knew a man who did.

My next job was to dispose of the 'not so pleasant' bundle in the car boot. I checked my watch. 10.45pm. Still a bit early.So, with some time to kill; I drove the 10 miles or so to the nearest service station. I could do with topping up the fuel anyway. I had a few cups of black coffee over the 'I' crossword, which I still hadn't finished. I gave Em a quick call before it got too late. She told me that Davey's funeral was in two day's time. The day after my wife's. 'You will come, Charlie won't you?' 'Of course, it would look strange if I didn't'. I wrote down the details on my newspaper and agreed to phone her in the morning to arrange things. We said our goodnights. Before putting my phone in my pocket I turned it off. I picked up my paper and went out to the car. Driving the short distance from the restaurant area to the garage forecourt, I filled up with petrol.

Slightly before midnight I parked up, just beyond the cemetery. Popping the boot I grabbed the spade, rope and roll of binliners and headed for the small group of trees I'd seen earlier. Behind the trees was a freshly-dug grave. It had been lined with a green material, a bit like artificial grass. It reminded me of the stuff you see on shelves in greengrocer's shops. I carefully removed it. I looked down into the hole in the ground. Some poor bastard's final resting place. Then a thought occurred to me. No. Surely not. I couldn't help feeling how funny that would be though.

Chapter forty seven

I dropped the spade and the bin liners into the hole. Tying the rope around a near-by headstone I lowered myself down. As quickly and quietly as I could I began digging, putting the soil into the bin bags. When I'd filled eight bags I decided that was enough. I tied a bag of soil to the end of the rope I then climbed out and pulled the bag out after me. I went back five more times and repeated the process. With all but two of the bags removed I sat for a minute to get my breath back.

I went to the car, and deciding it was too far to carry Czeckov, I took a chance and drove up alongside the grave. I lifted him out of the boot and hid him, among the trees, while I drove the car on out of the cemetery. Parking up on the road I jogged back to the grave. I was just about to drag him to his final resting place when I heard voices. I froze. At first it had sounded like they were coming through the graveyard, but as the voices faded. I realised it was just a couple of drunks walking along the main road. When I could no longer hear them I dragged Czeckov from the bushes and rolled him into the hole. I jumped down next to him and scattered the two bags of soil around him. Climbing out I emptied four more bags down onto him and he completely vanished. I replaced the green liner and surveyed my handywork.Looked fine to me.I emptied the remaining bags of soil on the mound beside the grave. Checking I hadn't left anything behind I picked up the rope, spade and bin bags and jogged back to the car. I was covered in mud.Especially my trainers. I lit a fag and spent a few minutes cleaning myself up, then drove the short distance back to the B&B. When I got out of the car I realised I'd got quite a bit of mud on the carpets. Sod it. I'd get it valeted before I returned it. Up in my room I threw all my muddy clothes in the bath then got in. Closing the curtain, I turned on the shower. As I showered I worked the mud out of my clothes with my feet.

Tonight I'd managed to tie up all of my loose ends.Except for one. John Kenny.

Tomorrow he'd get his.

Chapter forty eight

The next morning, before breakfast I put on my running kit and went for a jog. My trainers were still a bit damp but heh, I wasn't running a marathon. Taking my usual route I slowed as I approached my previous night's handywork. Everything looked fine to me. Passing the two side-by-side graves a little further along, I thought again of what I'd actually done. I'd almost certainly buried Czeckov in my wife's grave. I must have. She was being buried here, this morning. The two graves next to each other were obviously for two relatives who'd wanted to be buried together. Unless they were burying Gross and the missus together! The other possibility is that they were going to dig her grave this morning. After all, her funeral wasn't until 11.15

Back at the B&B I had my fry-up then showered and got dressed in my suit.

The church service was fairly sparsely attended. Fewer still were at the cemetery. As she was lowered into the ground, on top of Czeckov I covered my face with my hands. To any onlookers I was trying to hide my grief. In reality I was trying not to pee myself laughing.

All I could think of was 'Typical Sally. Even in death you've managed to sneak a bloke in with you for an eternity of infidelity!'

Afterwards, back at the outlaw's, I showed my face for a while. After an hour of fake smiles and false grief I bade my farewells and did one.

I stopped at a pub the other side of their village. I ordered a pint and took it outside. I lit a cigarette and then phoned Em;

'Hi Charlie. How did it go?'

'Oh, you know, it was ok. Listen I want us to get the hell out of here asap.'

'South Africa?'

'You bet. I suggest we go tomorrow. After Davey's funeral.'

'Yes but what about jabs. Oh and my passport? Does Charlie need one? I'm not sure, all the rules have changed. God I don't think we can sort it that quickly.'

'Leave it to me, I'll sort it. All I need is your passport and a recent photo of Charlie.'

'My passport is at home dammit.'

'That's not a problem I'll get it for you. I need to collect Monty anyway. I'll pick it up for you tonight. Where is it?'

'It should be in the filo-fax, at the side of the sideboard, near Monty's tank.'

'Is it in date?'

'It should be for another 2 or 3 years.'

'Oh. The alarm. I set the alarm. It's 2627. The neighbour, Mrs Hogg has a spare key. I'll phone her and tell her to expect you.'

'No worries, 2627. Take Charlie to one of those photo booths. Do it today. I'll collect the photos from you bright and early in the morning.' Davey's funeral was at 2.30pm. I should be back in time. 'One last thing, I don't have pen and paper. Txt me all of Charlie's details, place and date of birth, middle name etc.'

'Will do Charlie. Take care.'

'Always.' I said. I hung up and speed-dialled Frank.

Chapter forty nine

He answered straight away.

'Charlie. I don't see or hear from you for months on end, then twice in a week. What's up?'

I hated talking on the phone but didn't have a lot of choice in the matter.

'I need some travel docs. Two amending and one new one. I've got the photos. All old type on the docs. I need to get everything to you in the morning and pick up again the next day.'

'You don't want much do you? It can be done but it'll be pricey.'

'I've got a good part-ex for you. The hand-held I got from you last week plus four more. Usual meet at 10.00. I'll phone if I'm running late.'

'No worries Charlie. See you in the morning.'

Chapter fifty

I drove slowly past Em's house. Everything seemed ok. There were no suspicious looking vans parked nearby. At the end of the road I did a u-turn and parked up with her house in sight. I lit a cig. It had been a few days since the gunmen had payed their unwelcome visit. If any of their friends had come snooping around they would've done so soon after they fell off the radar. They would've seen the house was empty and assumed we were unlikely to come back in a hurry. I put out my cig and drove up to the house. I knocked on the neighbour's door. Mrs 'Wotsit' opened the door with a smile.

'You must be Charlie.'

'That's me' I said, taking the offered key.

'I'll just grab a few things and pop the key back to you.' I said hurrying away. I could tell she wanted to catch up on some gossip and I had neither the time nor the inclination to get involved.As I turned the key and opened the door the alarm started to beep. I opened the cupboard and punched the code into the control panel. The beeping stopped. I stood still for a moment. Everything seemed normal. I went through to the kitchen and checked that the back door was still locked. It was. As I checked around the house all of the windows were secure. Taking Monty's bag from my pocket, I reached into his tank and got a hold on him. I lowered him into his bag and pulled the draw-string tight. Laying him down near the door, I turned my attention to the filo-fax. I quickly located Em's passport. It was with Davey's. I pocketed both. I also found Davey's driving licence. I took that aswell. Grabbing Monty I reset the alarm and left. I dropped the key through next-door's letter box.As I said. I didn't fancy a chat.

Chapter fifty one

I arrived at my B&B at 7.30pm. I went up to my room and changed into dark clothing. Twenty minutes later I was back in the car heading for the abandoned farm buildings on the track behind Kenny's house. I parked the car in one of them. I took Monty out of his bag and hung him around my neck. It would be easier to carry him that way. I had about half a mile to go over fields to JK's house. I checked that I had my cigarette lighter. I wasn't planning on stopping for a fag. Although Monty was nowhere near fully grown, if he began constricting I wouldn't be able to stop him. I'd never had cause to do it but I'd been told by a man who knew snakes that a quick blast on his nose with a cigarette lighter would stop him constricting.

It was a dark night. No moon. I climbed the low fence into the fields that backed onto JK's housing estate. Sticking to the hedge that bordered the main road, I made my way towards my marker, clearly defined against the skyline were the telegraph poles.

The hedge provided me with cover but also shielded my eyes from the car headlights, thus keeping my night-vision relatively unimpaired.

Before long I'd reached the row of telegraph poles. I progressed along the row of garden hedges that the overhead cables followed, until I came to the forth pole. I carefully made my way through a gap in the hedge and found myself in JK's garden. It was a fairly small garden. From where I crouched near the hedge I had a perfect view of the house. It was lit up like a Christmas tree. I could see JK sitting in his lounge. He was watching a ridiculously large wide-screen TV. To his right, in the kitchen, I could see two women and a young toddler his wife, daughter and grandchild? Probably.

Keeping to the shadows I made my way along the side of the house, down a narrow alleyway, I found myself behind JK's truck. He was a creature of habit. He always arrived at the pub at 9.40pm. That meant he must leave his house just after 9.30pm. I checked my watch. The luminous dial showed 8.58pm. I sat back in the shadows to wait.

It's hard to explain, but there's a certain place your mind goes when you are waiting. I'd done it many times. This was a piece of cake compared to some of the times I'd had to wait. In the past I'd lain in a small hollow in the ground for days. Eating sleeping (well cat-napping) and even shitting in a bag where I lay. You kind of relax but don't. Your senses become hightened. You can hear a pin drop. You spot the slightest movement, even in your peripheral vision. You become totally focused on the mission, and yet you are in a kind of peaceful place. Then Action!

Chapter fifty two

At 9.05pm the front door of the house opened. There was a sudden 'thoop' as the central locking was operated, the hazards simultaneously flashing.Shit.Why so early? He was walking towards the truck. I got ready to strike. My plan was to wait for him to get in the drivers seat. I would then jump in the rear passenger seat behind him and drop Monty on his lap. Hopefully the shock would have the desired effect. If not I'd put my 9mm to his head and force him to drive. All of that now went out of the window as he opened the rear passenger door and held it while the young woman strapped the toddler in a child seat. She then got in the front and JK made his way round the bonnet, and got in the driver's seat. I just stayed put in the shadows and watched as he started the engine and drove off, presumably to give the woman and kid a lift home.
Shit! I wanted him dead but I wasn't going to risk the woman and her child. I slid back through the shadows to the garden, through the hedge and back across the fields to my car. Kenny would live to fight another day. Meanwhile I had another job to do.
I put Monty back in his bag and popped the car boot. Putting the snake in, I took out the shovel. I went around the back of the

sheds and removing the rocks I dug up the bin liners. I'd originally buried the weapons because I didn't want to be carrying them around more than necessary. I'd buried the money for safe keeping. Things had changed. I was going to part-exchange the hand guns with Davey against the cost of the passports. I was now planning on going to South Africa so would need to take the cash with me.

As I began to fill in the hole I changed my mind again. I slit open one of the 25k bundles of notes and put £1000 into a bin bag, along with one of the PPK's. I buried the bag and replaced the rocks. I was leaving the country, but if I came back I may well need some cash and a weapon in a hurry. Checking that I hadn't left anything behind, I got back in the car and drove to the B&B. I showered then phoned Em to make arrangements for the next day. Before going to bed I sorted out all my kit. I had an early start so didn't want to be pissing about first thing in the morning. I counted out a grand and put the stack of crisp 'nifties' into an envelope.

Chapter fifty three

At just after 7.30am I pulled up at the corner shop near Em's parents' house. She got in the car next to me and gave me a hug. 'Missed you.' She said grabbing my cheeks in both hands and smothering my face in kisses. 'Missed you too. How's the sprog?'
'Oh he's fine. I can't wait for this afternoon. Not the funeral, I'm not looking forward to that. No. I can't wait to go away with you. My mum and dad are sweet but they're starting to get on my tits.'
'Not long now babe. Have you got the photos? Cause I really am in a bit of a hurry.'
She gave them to me and after another bombardment of kisses she got out of the car. I waved as I set off to the big smoke.
At just before 9 00am I pulled into a motorway services. I had some passport photos done of myself. As I waited for them to develop I speed-dialled Frank and told him I was on time. It wouldn't really matter if I got caught in traffic and was a little late. He wouldn't be hanging around a tube station carrying anything 'dodgy' like the last time we'd met. This time he would be there to collect the 'dodgy' gear. My photos popped out.

I was hungry so went to get something to eat. As I stood in a short queue, waiting to place my order I scrolled through the contacts on my phone and rang 'Dinger'.

I'd first met Major 'Dinger' Bell when he was a warrant officer. I was on a refresher course. Soon after, he'd been posted to some 'secret squirrel' branch of military intelligence. He was fluent in several languages, particularly Russian. He'd tried to persuade me to take up a language, but to be honest it hadn't appealed to me. 'These days, of course you need to be learning Arabic or Chinese.' He'd predicted.

I still bumped into him from time to time. He'd long since retired and didn't live far from me. Having said that, I more often than not saw him at funerals. That was the reason for my call to him now. After the normal chit-chat I asked him if he would be at Davey's funeral that afternoon. He confirmed that he would. I said that I had something I'd like him to look at and translate for me. 'Intruiging.I shall look forward to it.' He'd said.

Chapter fifty four

Eating my 'Big Mac' meal as I drove I made good time into London. Frank, as usual was on timeI stopped briefly at the kerbside and he jumped in.
I passed him the passports, both sets of photos and Davey's driving licence.
'Ok Frank I want my photo on the man's passport and driving licence and I need a new passport for the kid.'
'What name?' He asked. I glanced down in the footwell at my empty take away carton.
'Mcdonald. On all of them, including the woman's.' I said.
'No worries mate. These old passports are a piece of piss compared to the new ones.'He put them in his pocket.
'Down at your feet are four pistols. I changed my mind and kept one. You'll need to wipe them down. I buried them for safe-keeping so they've had a good blast of WD40.'
He looked into the bag. 'Take it you've checked them over Charlie?' 'Yea mate they're good.' He put the bin liner in a canvas bag that he'd brought with him.I passed him the envelope and he flicked through the notes.

'That cover it?' I asked him. He smiled and said 'Yep. It's a deal.'
'I need to meet you back here tomorrow for the docs. Not sure of the time yet but it'll be around midday.' I'd completed a lap of the square and pulled over and let Frank out almost at the same spot where I'd picked him up minutes earlier.
'Laters.' He said as he hopped out. Looking in my mirror as I pulled into the traffic I saw him disappear into the crowd outside the tube station.

Chapter fifty five

I made good time through the London traffic. I checked my watch and realised I had time to make a few stops on my way back to the B&B. The first was one of curiosity. I was approaching the lay—by where I'd torched the 'Merc' a few days ago. Unfortunately I was going the wrong way. It looked open and I could see several cars through the trees. I carried on to the next roundabout and doing a 360 drove back to the lay by and pulled in. As I drove slowly to where the 'Merc' had been I noticed some fresh tarmac. The nearby trees showed signs of having been on fire. They'd obviously done a rush job to get the lay by up and running, due to all the trucks that stop there at night. Up ahead the café had several boarded up windows but otherwise looked unscathed. The owner seemed to be doing a roaring trade, judging by the queue of customers waiting to be served. I'd obviously helped his business. I didn't feel quite so bad about his gas bottle and cooking oil now!

One last stop on the way to fill up with fuel. As I paid I grabbed a 'sarnie' from the fridge near the till. Driving always made me hungry. God forbid I ever had a job driving for a living. I'd end up the size of John Kenny.

Chapter fifty six

Back at the B&B I showered and put my suit on. I then spent almost an hour on my lap top booking flights to South Africa. Taking my last few bits and pieces from the room I went to the reception desk and settled my bill. I then went outside and stood near the hire car and waited for Em. I'd just lit a cig as she pulled up next to me. She looked very refined all in black. I tapped on the rear window at little Charlie, who also looked quite dapper in his little suit. He grinned. 'Open your boot Em so I can dump my gear in.' I transferred everything from my boot to hers. A quick check of my car to make sure I hadn't left anything, then I took the keys into the B&B where I left them for whoever came to collect the car. As Em drove us to the church I phoned the rental company and told them where they could collect their car.

The service and burial were well attended. More friends than family. As far as anyone knew Davey didn't have any relatives. At the burial, standing alongside several uniformed colleagues of Davey's from his old regiment, I spotted Dinger. As people began to leave I spoke with him briefly. Em was deep in conversation with someone so I mimed 'key' to her. She rooted through her bag and passed me the car key without breaking sentence. I led Dinger out to the road where we'd parked. I opened the boot of

Black Heart

the hire car and gave him a carrier bag containing the three Russians' phones. 'Not telling you how to suck eggs, but don't fire these up with the SIM cards in.' He gave me a look that said 'Stupid boy!' He asked how I'd come by them. I told him I'd rather not say.
'Ok Charlie. I'll have a look at them later. The missus is out playing bridge tonight so it'll give me something to do. I'll phone you if I find anything interesting.' He left and I wandered back to find Em and Charlie.
After drinks and a buffet at Ems parents' we finally set off for the airport.

Chapter fifty seven

At just after 10.00pm that night we checked into our hotel at Heathrow airport. Once Em had got Charlie off to sleep we sat with a bottle of red wine, glasses this time, and I filled her in on the arrangements. 'Tomorrow night at 9.45pm we fly from here on an Air France flight to Johannesberg via Paris. We will be picked up the next morning by a friend of mine. We'll stay at his place until we decide what to do long-term.'

'Sounds wonderful, I can't wait.'

'Before that though, I've got a lot of things to do.' She gave me a suspicious look.

'Don't start. It's nothing 'dodgy'. I have to go and see a friend and collect our passports. I've got a few things in your hire car that I need to lose.(No bodies at least!)Then I'm going to leave the hire car somewhere else and get a train back. We're not travelling under our names but even so I don't want the car being collected from here. Before you ask, as far as I know we are in the clear and nobody should be after us. Hey, the less of a trail we leave the better. Oh and we are now officially Mr, Mrs and Master Mcdonald.'

'That's got a nice ring to it actually, Mrs Emma Mcdonald.'
'Yes I thought.Could've been Emma Kentucky-Fried-Chicken. Hyphonated, don't you know!'
Then she said 'Mr and Mrs.Is that a proposal?' Before I had to answer that particular awkward question I noticed a funny noise. It took a second or two for me to register what it was. It was my cellphone. It was on silent mode. What I could hear was it vibrating in my jacket, which was lying on the dressing table. I took it out. Three missed calls, all from Dinger.
I rang him and he answered immediately.
'Sorry Dinger. I put my phone on silent at the funeral and forgot to re-set it. What's up?'
'We need to talk Charlie. Come over to my place now. You know where I live.'
'It's a bit late now Dinger.'
'Ok 07.00 Tomorrow.' That was an order not a request. Something was wrong.
'Make it 09.00 Dinger I'm in Manchester' I lied.
'Ok 09.00 on the dot!' With that he hung up. Something was definitely wrong!
'Manchester?' Said Em.

Chapter fifty eight

'Fuck it.' I said under my breath.

'Problem?' asked Em.

'To be honest I don't know.' I said sitting her down on the bed and taking her hand.

'Honest? I'm not sure I like the way lies fly off of your tongue Charlie. Why did you just tell whoever that was that you were in Manchester?'

'Force of habit.From now on Em we need to be careful what we tell people. Everything has to be on a 'need to know' basis. In other words, if someone doesn't need to know something, then we don't tell them. That was a friend of mine on the phone. He's got some information for me.About who those Russians were by the way. Only problem is I now have to drive up to friggin Oxford tomorrow to speak to him. Like I said, he's a friend. But he doesn't need to know I'm at heathrow. He also doesn't need to know that I, sorry we, are off to South Africa tomorrow night. What have you told your parents by the way?'

'Nothing Charlie.I just said me and little Charlie were going away for a while. I think she knows though. About us I mean.

Black Heart

Don't worry, she likes you. At the end of the day she will just want me to be happy. You make me happy Charlie and I can't hide that, not from my mum anyway. Yeah, she's not daft, she knows.'

'Well it would have to come out sooner or later I suppose.'

'Don't worry Charlie. Like I said, she will just want us to be happy.'

'Yeah I'm sure you're right. Now get your kit off Mrs Mcdonald, I've got an early start in the morning!'

Chapter fifty nine

I slipped out of the room at just before 06.00. In the restaurant, which wasn't open yet, I managed to get a few cups of black coffee and some toast. I smothered the toast in Marmite. Yep, I loved it.

On the way to Dingers I phoned Frank. It sounded like I'd woke him up.

'Did I wake you mate?'

'No Charlie.' He lied yawning. 'What's up?'

'Is everything sorted?'

'Shouldn't be a problem.I'm picking up your items on the way to our meet.'

'Ok I'm not sure what time I'm going to be there. Something came up. I'll ring when I have a definite ETA. Oh and I have a favour to ask. Do you know anyone who can look after a snake for me?'

'A what?' I told him about Monty. I said I'd pay £500 to somebody to look after him for me until I could collect him.

'Leave it with me Charlie.A six foot fucking python.Fucks sake.'

'Fucks snake!' I said, hanging up.

Talking of Monty reminded me of JK. I felt like driving round to his house and emptying my 9mm into him. Much as I'd love to, I unfortunately couldn't. Not today anyway. Besides I had to get rid of the weapon. I couldn't exactly check-in at the airport with it.

At just before 09.00 I pulled up outside Dinger's house. I rang the bell and he answered. Sending his wife off to make coffee, he led me through to his conservatory.

'Charlie, son. You've opened a 'can of worms' here, and no mistake.'

Chapter sixty

'Charlie I know you're not going to tell me how you came across these phones. But the fact that you gave them to me tells me it wasn't 'officially.' Charlie I'm duty-bound to hand all of this to our boys. I should've done so already.' He jestured at piles of paper on his computer desk Page after page of phone numbers? Longer looking numbers and txt messages that had been transcribed in Russian and then translated into English.
'So what are we looking at Dinger?' I asked him. He hesitated.
'Come on Dinger. If the shit's going to hit the fan, I should at least know why.'
'I've only just scraped the surface and I've been working on it all night. A lot of these longer-looking numbers I suspect are encrypted. Codes aren't my department. All I know is that they are offshore bank accounts.Hundreds of them.'
Just then his wife came in, carrying a tray of coffee and biscuits. She smiled and placing the tray on a table, left without a word. She obviously knew a chat was not on the cards.
'These two phones,' he continued, as soon as his wife left.
'Belonged to two employees from the Russian embassy. They

Black Heart

were called Ilya Lysenko and Boris Shkurenev. That was easy enough to deduce as they both had each others names and numbers in each others contact lists.If you follow?' I nodded. 'Now this one, the one with all the encrypted numbers.This belonged to a man called Vladimir Czechov.He's referred to by the other two,who'd been looking for him, as 'The Accountant.' Apparently he has vanished and the shit has hit the proverbial. The world and his dog are looking for him.Including these two. Now our man Czeckov is holding upwards of $500m of mob money, presumably in the offshore accounts I just told you about and naturally his disappearance is causing a bit of a panic. I take it you know something of his whereabouts as you gave me his phone.'

Ignoring that last comment I asked him 'So what's the 500 big ones for? Are they saving for a rainy day?'

'That's the scary bit Charlie.The baddies are 'upping the ante.' Why bother bribing coppers or DAs? These bad boys are 'thinking outside the box.' They are going to do the totally unexpected. They've clubbed together enough money to run their own candidate.'

'What? You don't mean?'

'That's exactly what I mean Charlie. The Russian mafia are running their own candidate for the top job.President of the United States of America!'

Chapter sixty one

En route to my RV with Frank I made a quick detour to my house. I needed a few t-shirts and my 'crocs' for my trip to South Africa. More importantly I needed to stash my service pistol. I'd toyed with the idea of going to the barns and burying it alongside the other one and the cash. I decided against that idea. It would be risky in broad daylight. True I'D dumped Czeckov there in daylight but that had been a necessity and it was literally an in out job. I'd been there twice in one day, but in two different vehicles, which wasn't so bad. I was in yet another car now. No.I didn't want to push my luck with that particular location. I had a 'get out of jail free card' stashed there.

Letting myself into the house I picked up the mail.Nothing interesting. Upstairs I grabbed the few bits and pieces for my trip. Opening the safe in my wardrobe I put my Browning 9mm high power inside and locked it. That's when my phone rang.My work phone. Dammit, Dinger had thrown me to the lions. The only good thing about the call is that I'd received it here. I waited for the ringing to stop, then I pulled up Frank's number and typed it into my other phone. I turned off my work phone, took off the battery and left the phone pieces on the table in the hall as I went out to the car with my things. Popping the boot I took out the shovel, bin bags, rope and WD40 and put them in my garden shed. Back at the car I put Monty in the front passenger footwell. Counting out 500 quid I put that in the glove box. I lit a fag and sat for a minute. Was that everything? Yep, I couldn't think of anything else. Something was bugging me though. You know that feeling that you've forgotten something? I had that feeling now. Actually I'd had the feeling since I was at Dinger's.

The feeling was still with me as I pulled away from my house. Well it was 'my house' at the minute. I noticed the 'For Sale' sign as I drove off.

Just before I joined the M4 I pressed dial on my phone.

Frank took a while to answer, presumeably because he hadn't recognised the number on the incoming call.

Chapter sixty two

Frank answered.

'Hi mate it's Charlie.New phone. I'm now on the M4.Should be about 2hrs depending on the traffic.You can save this as my new number. I'll give you a ring when I'm almost with you, ok?'

'No worries Charlie. Oh, and I've got someone to do the snake thing.'

'Good see you soon.' I hung up and rang Em. (Yes, I know but using a mobile phone while driving seemed a bit trivial compared to some of the shit I'd done recently. Besides I was in a hurry. At least, if I got pulled over, I no longer had a body in the boot!)

'Hi Charlie are you on your way? I can tell you're in a car.'

'Slight change of plan babe.'

There was no way that I could hang around at Heathrow until 9.45 tonight. I had to get out of the country asap. My boss had called me. I hadn't answered the call. He would send someone to the B&B. Next they would probably check my house. I reckoned I had about 3 hours before they would start the search in earnest. It was going to be tight but I thought I had just enough time to leave the country.

'Em you and Charlie need to get the train from Heathrow to Paddington. They're every 15 minutes or so. Bring my kit with you. From Paddington get the tube to St Pancras. I'll meet you there and give you your passports. Just check first, you might be able to go direct from Heathrow to St Pancras, probably not such a regular service though.'
'Charlie what's happening?'
'Nothing to worry about Em. I just need to go as soon as possible. Don't worry it's not the Russians. It's my own people. They're looking for me.'
'Are you AWOL or something?'
'No Em. How can I be? I'm on compassionate leave. No it's nothing major, except it'll involve days of questions and I can't be arsed, we're off on our hols. I'm still flying to SA with you; I'm just missing out the first leg. I'll be meeting you in Paris.'
'Do I need to leave now? What about my luggage? I'm getting confused Charlie.'
'Calm down Em. You've got plenty of time. You need to be at St Pancras in 2 hours. Buy return tickets. You are just going to meet me and give me my bags. I will give you the passports and you will then go back to Heathrow. You'll then have loads of time to do your duty-free shopping and check in for your flight. Ok babe? Think of it as an adventure. See you soon.'

Chapter sixty three

As I approached our meeting place I could see Frank and a younger guy waiting at the kerb. I'd phoned him and told him when I was about half an hour away. I pulled up along side them and got out of the car. 'You drive Frank' I said jumping into the front passenger seat. He got in and his mate got in behind me. As Frank pulled out into the traffic he said 'Where to? This is my kid brother Harry by the way.'
'St Pancras.' Then turning to Harry 'Pleased to meet you Harry. I take it you're the snake man, have you handled them before?'
'Yeah mate I worked at a petting zoo place when I was a kid. I loved the snakes, most of the others refused to go near 'em so I used to take care of 'em. Mum wouldn't let me have one, but I've always wanted one. Where is he, can I see him?' I passed Monty up and over my head to Harry. He opened the bag and got him out.
'Cool. He's lovely, what's his name? Tell me it's not Monty 'cause that would be so predictable an' uncool?'
'Call him what you like mate, he's yours for the predictable' I said to hide my 'un-coolness.' 'Here, babysitting fees.'
I passed him the money from the glove box. 'Have you got a tank for him?'

'In the pipeline, just bought one on e-bay, we're picking it up this afternoon.'
Frank handed me the passports and I checked them over.
'Nice one Frank. One last favour.' We were approaching St Pancras. 'Can you drop me at the station and take the car back for me? It's payed for 'till tomorrow. Keep it today if you like. Just drop it at the nearest Avis place by tomorrow evening. Also there's a pretty new child seat in the back that's going begging'
'No worries Charlie. Hey and thanks for the kiddie's seat, my missus has been nagging at me to get a new one.'
The traffic lights were on red. Grabbing my bag I opened the door.
'This'll do me Frank. Take care, you too Harry.' I got out before the lights changed and walked into the station.

Chapter sixty four

I paid for my ticket on the Euro-star to Paris. I took out my phone and was just about to phone Em, when I saw her and Charlie approaching. 'That was good timing. Have you just got here?' 'Yes.' She said, a little out of breath. 'I got here as quickly as I could but I missed a tube and was worried you'd be waiting and.' 'Em, I only just got here myself. Relax. Come let's get a coffee.' I took Charlie from her and carried him to a nearby table. I went and got us some coffees and dohnuts. I got Charlie an orange juice. Back at the table I gave Em her passports and took my holdall.

She still wasn't too happy about me going on ahead but I told her I had to. Besides we would be harder to trace doing it this way. There was a funny smell eminating from Charlie. While Em took him to the loos to change his nappy I made a call to my travel agents. I told them that I would now be joining the Jo'berg flight at Paris but the other two members of my party would be travelling from LHR as booked. I couldn't believe the fuckers actually charged me 60quid for NOT taking the first leg of the flight. I'd bet they were busy selling my empty seat to Paris, even as I gave her my card details for the charge. As I hung up Em and

Charlie returned. She obviously thought something was wrong by the look on my face. 'I'm fine Em.Frigging travel agents. Robbing gits. At least Dick Turpin wore a mask!' After a few sips of coffee I asked Em what she'd done with her cash. 'It's in here.' She said tapping her shoulder-bag. I told her to split it up and spread it out amongst her and Charlie's baggage. Finishing my coffee I checked my watch. 'Time I wasn't here Em.' I gave her a kiss. See you in Paris about midnight.'

'You're such a romantic Charlie.Paris at midnight!'

Chapter sixty five

I sat on the Paris-bound Euro-Star.I couldn't decide what to do. Something was 'niggling'at me. I knew it was risky to make the call, but if I didn't do it before I left the country it would be difficult to pass on what I knew without giving my location away. I made the call. His wife answered. She told me he was sleeping. He'd been up all night.

I told her who I was and that he would want to take my call. I said I would ring back in 5 minutes and hung up.

Memory varies from person to person. I personally have a shit memory for names. I'm terrible, always have been. Faces I'm much better at. I can't for the life of me put a bloody name to it, but I tend to remember someone's face.Numbers. Now you're talking. I am very good at remembering numbers. Before we all got mobile phones and home phones had programmable address books things were different. We all stored phone numbers in diaries or address books. I didn't. I remembered them. I don't know how. I sort of make a rhyme out of the digits and, well remember them!

That morning as I'd sat opposite Dinger I'd recognised a phone number. Even reading upside down I'd noticed the same number appeared, on several occasions, on the two separate piles of data that related to the phones belonging to the two Russians, who I'd shot at Em's. (See I've forgotten their names!) No doubt 'the office' would put the pieces together, but if I knew something it was still my duty to tell them.

I pressed re-dial. This time Dinger answered. 'Charlie, what's up?'

'Have you still got the transcripts from the Russian's phones?' I asked, knowing the answer would be in the negative.

'No. I gave everything I had to your guys. Why?'

'Thought you would.Do you remember seeing the name Dimitri on any of the phones.In address books or in txt messages?' He thought for a moment.

'No sorry. Why, who is he? Why aren't you having this conversation with your own people?' He was right of course, but I had a plane to catch.

'I'm on leave.' I told him.

'Write this number down and give it to the office. Tell them to check Dimitri and also that I think he is working for 'Red'.I gave him the number. 'Repeat that back to me Dinger.'

Black Heart

He did and I said 'Adios Amigo.' I hung up. Hopefully I'd thrown him a 'red herring' with my Spanish farewell.

Chapter sixty six

The train journey was fine. I had a few beers and the 90 minutes to France seemed to fly by. Almost before I knew it we were pulling into Gar Du Nord. I put my watch forward 1hour. It was just after 4pm local. I had until 10pm to get to Charles De Gaulle and check-in. I wandered round for a while eventually I settled at a table and ordered a beer and a sandwich. Twelve friggin' euros! I would have to change some more money. I needed enough to keep me going 'til I caught my flight. I also needed some change for the phone.

I found a Bureau de Change and getting ripped-off on the exchange rate, got some more euros. At a News stand I bought today's 'I'. That was another mistake.If I'd bought it the other side of the 'chunnel'it would've been a quarter the price. Still I now had something to pass the time. I also had some change to make a call to SA.

Putting my bags down at the pay-phone I dialled Jack's number. As I waited for my call to connect I just happened to see a hand slowly emerge from between my feet, reaching for the shoulder strap of my holdall. I stamped down hard on the offending digits with my right heel. 'Va tu fair Enculais' I said to the little shit in

my best pigeon-french. Lifting my foot and watching him 'leg it' away, cradling his sore hand. 'What?' Said Jack in my ear.
'Oh. Hi mate. Not you. I was 'explaining' to a bloody pick-pocket.'
'Your French is even worse than your Afrikaans. What time are you arriving then Charlie, and who's this new lady of yours?' I chatted with him for a while. I gave him our flight details, and a severely edited background on mine and Em's relationship. I hung up and went in search of my connection to the airport.

Chapter sixty seven

At the airport time started to drag. It had been a long day. I'd been rushing around all over the place but ever since I'd boarded the train I'd been sitting around 'twiddling my thumbs'. I'd collected my ticket and boarding card and when the gate opened at 10.00pm had checked in for my flight. Em and Charlie should be here in about an hour, and an hour after that we would be on our way. I'd finished my crossword, the word ladders and the codeword. As I sat drinking yet another coffee my mind drifted to what Dinger had discovered from the phones. I now knew why Czechov had to disappear. Why his body couldn't be found. He had access to $500million.of mob money. They needed it to fund their man's presidential campaign. If he died then presumeably his next of kin would get their hands on the money, and killing him would've been no more than an inconvenience. But without a body, how could they prove he was dead? It would stop the n-o-k getting the money and the whole campaign would grind to a halt. I understood WHY I'd been hired. But WHO had hired me? Dimitri had been the front man. But for who? Was he working for the US government, ie 'officially'? Or was he working for Red? Ie 'unofficially?' My money was on the latter, and here's why.

Officially the various US agencies wouldn't want a guy in the pocket of the mafia becoming the most powerful man in America, the world probably. But surely they would have got hold of Czeckov and 'questioned' him. Thus stopping the conspiracy and also confiscating the money? It would've been a major publicity coup for the current administration. I could picture the newspaper headlines 'Good Guys sieze $500m from the bad guys and use it to build two new hospitals blah blah.' To me that is how it would have gone. On the other hand Red would also want the plan scuppered. He was more powerful than all the other mobsters put together. He certainly would've felt threatened by what could happen. He would want Czeckov dead. But why wouldn't he want to get his hands on the money as well? I was now busy sinking my own theory. Maybe he just didn't have the resources to crack all the codes etc to get to the money? Surely he wouldn't be averse to torture? For whatever reason he'd decided on the disappearance route. That, at least for the moment, was my theory. I was interrupted from my thoughts by Em and Charlie's arrival. We all had a big hug.

Chapter sixty eight

During the 10hour flight to Jo'berg I told Em some of what awaited her. She was like a kid in a sweet shop. Talk about excited. All the stories I told her couldn't prepare her for what she had in store. I love South Africa. It was almost impossible to describe. I'd always dreamed of settling down there, ever since my first visit.

I'd first gone there for some 'R&R' back in 1989. I'd been based in South West Africa (now Namibia) as the Angolan bush war came to an end. I'd had a great time in SA and couldn't wait to go back. I got another chance in 2000. Mugabe had kicked off again in Zimbabwe (formerly Rhodesia) and I managed to spend some time across the border in SA before flying back to the UK. I managed a few more holidays over there and had seen KZN, having flown to Durban. I'd spent a few days being a 'surfin dude' and had then hired a car and done the 'garden route'. I'd also driven up through the Free State and had finally had a few days at Sun City in North West province. That was where I first met Jack and Karen. They were both ex-pats and had been in SA for about 20years. Jack was originally from Bolton. Karen was from Welsh Wales (apart from that she was fine!) We hit it off straight away and had a hell of a few days. So much so that I overslept and missed my coach to the airport. Jack and Karen had come to check out and seeing my predicament, Jack hadn't hesitated to offer me a lift. Brilliant people, they all were over there. Jack and Karen had a small lodge in the middle of nowhere and they invited me out to stay whenever I wanted. I'd managed to get over there a couple of times in the intervening years and was now on my way back there for a third time. I couldn't wait.

Chapter sixty nine

As usual, passport control took an age to get through. Once past there, the baggage re-claim went quite smoothly, and we were greeted by Jack as we exited the arrivals lounge.
'Hi Jack.' (Shouldn't say that too loud at an airport!) 'Am I glad to see you? This is Emma and little Charlie.' I couldn't help notice him raise an eyebrow slightly. Wiley old fox. He
Shook Em's hand and tweeked Charlie's cheek then led us out to the car park. The heat hit us as soon as we ventured out into the open. It was already hot and it was only mid morning. 'Drink?' Asked Jack, as we got into his mini-bus. He took the lid off his mobile bar (a large cool-box full of beer and cokes, surrounded by ice cubes.) I took a Windhoek (imported Namibian beer) Em said she'd like a coke. Jack ignored her and gave her a beer. He then poured himself a whisky in a crystal glass, dropped in a few ice cubes, and added a splash of coke.
'Cheers all. Welcome to South Africa.' 'Cheers.' we said clinking bottles and glass.
Concidering Jack's place was in the middle of nowhere, I always found it amazing that he was only an hour from Jo'berg airport.

Well it could be triple that if the traffic was bad. You haven't seen tail-backs 'till you've been to Jo'berg.

This morning though, the traffic was flowing smoothly.

Jack's lodge was smack bang in the middle of 'The cradle of Humankind', a World Heritage site. Once past the nearest little town Muldersdrif, it was good bye to tarmac.Dirt roads from now on. The bumpy road woke Charlie up. In fairness he'd been a little super star. He'd been a bit of a pain at Paris, but he had been tired and bored. Once on the aircraft he'd slept a lot of the journey and had been happy to scoff meals and watch in-flight movies when he was awake.

We pulled into the driveway, crossing the stream we headed uphill slightly to Kenjara lodge. As we parked up a couple of Jack's staff came out to help with our luggage. Jack led us to our room, via the bar! Em resisted the offer of a drink and instead took Charlie to the room. Over my third beer since landing in SA I filled Jack in on a few things. I thanked him for the room but said we were looking for somewhere nearby to rent and could be looking to buy. He said he'd ask around. I also told him that if anyone was asking for us, we weren't here.

'Have you eloped together or something Charlie? Seriously, are you in some kind of trouble?'
'No nothing like that we both just need a break' I told him about Sally. He didn't seem too bothered. He'd only ever met her once and I don't think they'd hit it off. I said Em had recently lost her husband. Vague. I certainly wasn't going to tell him how.

Chapter seventy

'Another one?' Asked Jack.

'No ta' I said. 'I'd better go and have a shower.'

Ignoring me, Jack opened me another beer and poured himself a scotch.

'Nothing changes here at 'the evil place' I see. I'll get these. Can you start me a tab? I've got no Rand. You still in the market for sterling?' Jack, like many white South Africans was a bit twitchy at the moment. Having seen what had happened in neighbouring Zimbabwe and the resulting effect on the Zim' dollar, he was always keen to convert Rand to pounds sterling.

'You bet. I'll take all you've got.' I doubted that! 'I've got about £2000.' I lied.

'Ok I'll sort that out later. Lils will be in tonight. I seem to remember her saying something recently about house-sitting, and for some reason she can't do it. That could be a short-term solution to accommodation for you guys. Not that you're not welcome here.'

House-sitting in SA was big business. If you and your family went away for a few weeks holiday, leaving the property uninhabited, you would almost certainly return to an empty house. And I mean EMPTY. No belongings, no carpets, no light bulbs even. Lils had supplemented her allowance whilst going through college through her house-sitting; Lils wasn't her real name, by the way. That was my fault. When I'd first met her, years ago, she'd introduced herself to me as Lillian. Lil for short. She was Afrikaans and hadn't heard of the English word 'Lils', and its sexual connotations. If I remember correctly, I did get a slap from her when she found out, but it was too late. She was now known by everyone as Lils.

I managed to escape from the bar while Jack was on the phone, and headed to my room.

Freshened up and changed into swimming gear we all went out to the pool. Em plastered little Charlie in factor 45 and then rubbed some on my back. I did the rest of me and then did her back for her. We splashed around in the pool and lounged about in the sun. That's how Karen found us when she came back from work. She was surprised to see us.

Apparently, Jack hadn't told her that I'd phoned to say we were coming. She was delighted. Right up until I dumped her fully clothed, into the pool.

'You bastard Charlie!' 'Fair's fair. I owed you that from my last visit.' Although she personally hadn't thrown me in, she had orchestrated my ceremonial dunking.

Black Heart

I had probably deserved it. The England team, rugby I think, or it may have been cricket, were doing amazingly well on tour over here and I'd wound up a few of the locals. Hence my dunking. The South Africans are passionate about both rugby and cricket and have a serious sense of humour failure when things don't go to plan, ie if they lose.

We dossed around by the pool until it started to get dark, and then went to our room to get ready for dinner. Before going through to dinner I called Em out onto our balcony.

'What's wrong Charlie?'

'Nothing's wrong. Just sit here a minute and listen.'

'What am I listening for?'

'Be patient it'll be worth waiting for.' I lit us both a cig and passed one to her. Then it started. In the distance. Then slightly closer. Then practically outside our room. Then from almost everywhere, or so it seemed.

'What the . . . is that what I think?'

'Yep. Lions. Lots of them.' When you are close to roaring lions you don't just hear them. You can feel the vibrations in your chest. Rather like the throbbing of the bass at a disco.

'That is amazing. They sound really close though. They're not roaming loose out there are they?'

'No Em. Well yes, but they can't get to you here. The nearest ones are straight across the road from Jack's drive, literally about 1/2km from where we are sat. They belong to an ex-pat called Ken. I think he's got about 20. At least 2 of them live in his house with him. And his dogs! He's got a pair of cheetah as well. If you turn left out of Jack's drive, the land adjoining Ken belongs to a guy called Ed. He's got his own private collection of big cats. Lion, tiger, (Siberian and Bengalese) puma, lynx etc. Across the road from his property is the Lion and Rhino Nature Reserve, which he owns. There are two separate prides of lion on the reserve. We are quite literally surrounded by them. How cool is that?'

Chapter seventy one

Walking through to the bar it became obvious that, although Jack had kept our visit a secret from Karen, he'd certainly been busy telling everyone else. The bar was packed with just about everyone I'd ever met during my stays here.
'Fuck it this round's going to hurt! Set em up Jack. Put 'em on my tab, but first, give me 2 Windhoeks and an orange juice in here mate please.' I passed him Charlie's mug thingy with the lid on. In actual fact the round would cost next to nothing. Booze was ridiculously cheap over here. Besides, I wasn't short of a few quid. I made my way into the bar area, introducing Em to everyone as we went. Well everyone who's name I could remember that is. Ken was at the bar and introducing him to Em, I told her that this was the Ken who had the lions. Ken being Ken invited us round any time. We arranged to pop round the next day. Typical South Africa—'Yeh pop round and meet my lions!' Crazy!
Lils was there, with her new 'beau'. I gave her a big hug. I saw her more often in the UK than I did over here. She'd been working as a vet nurse at various surgeries in the UK and

whenever she was around she would give me a txt to arrange a visit. She kept me up to date on all the SA gossip. Mind you, now she was all 'loved up' I think her travelling days were over. Everyone gradually migrated outside for a braii. (Barbeque).As I queued up for some food I spoke to one of the game rangers from the Rhino Park.Nice guy, Afrikaans. I had no idea how to pronounce his name. I asked him the best place to get hold of a 9mm. Now if I'd asked that of anyone in the UK eyebrows would be raised, to say the least. Out here it was a perfectly normal question. Unfortunately, beautiful as it is, South Africa has a dark side.

Car-jackings and armed robberies were a common occurance. Not so prolific outside of the major cities. Still, most people I knew out here carried 'protection'. He said to leave it with him.

When the 'pass the pigs' started I grabbed Em by the arm and we legged it. That game had resulted in several serious hang-overs. Back at the room, while showering I told Em all about it.

'One drunken night at the bar, six or seven years ago myself, Lils Albert and a few other locals had turned a harmless family game into a very dangerous drinking game.

You threw the pigs as normal, but if you didn't stick and kept going, you were asking for trouble. If you 'bust' you had to drink. That involved necking a shooter. Then you had to make a rule.

The game went on and on with people having to drink and make a rule. Eventually you would get to a point, where, three sheets to the wind, you had to stand on one leg, hop anti-clockwise, drink with your 'pinkie' raised saying 'God save the Queen' etc etc. One mistake and you had to do the whole thing again. As I said a recipe for a hang-over.'

'Sounds mental. They seemed to take it very seriously.'

'Seriously? My God. A few years back someone actually stole the pigs. Could we find anywhere in SA that sold the game? No. And we tried everywhere. When I returned to the UK my first job was to trawl the toy shops and send a set to Jack. I am being deadly serious now; the pigs are kept in the safe!'

'You're joking?'

'Ask Jack or Karen tomorrow.'

After our shower we sat on our balcony and had a coffee and a cig. The lions were quiet, but the crickets were going for it. Other than the occasional laugh drifting from the bar it was very peaceful sat out in the African night. We sat there for several minutes enjoying the night. Then Em broke the silence. 'Now I know why you love Africa so much. Thanks for sharing it with us Charlie. I'm really glad you brought me and little Charlie with you.'

'Talking of which, we need to change his name to Chas or Chuck or Junior or something, save confusion.'

'Maybe.He's been good with all the travelling and stuff though, hasn't he?'

'Yep.I notice he's fast asleep. What did you say about taking advantage when he's asleep?'

'Oh Charlie, you're so demanding.' She said grabbing my hand and dragging me inside.

Chapter seventy one

We got up late the next morning.Once dressed we wandered through to the dining room.

A waitress appeared from the kitchen. We ordered coffee and Em helped herself to juice and cereal for her and Charlie. I didn't feel like anything to eat.Just coffee.Lots of it.

Eventually, after some nagging from Em, I forced myself to eat some toast and marmalade. We learned from the waitress that Miss Karen was at work and Mister Jack had gone shopping. About an hour later I was sat by the pool, drinking my fourth black coffee, when Jack returned. Em was sorting the nipper out.

'How are you this fine morning?' He asked me.

'Fine now.I was feeling a little fragile about four coffees back.'

Jack peed me off. He must've gone to bed hours after us and he'd sunk a whisky or two. Yet here he was, full of the joys of spring.

'You and Em need to put long sleeves and trousers on before we go over to Ken's. The cats can get a bit playful! Probably best if you don't take little Charlie.I'll get Precious to babysit him. We won't be there long.'

'Ok I'll go and tell Em, she's in the room now'.

Half an hour later, suitably dressed and minus little Charlie we got in Jack's truck. We'd left Charlie playing on the dining room floor with Precious, one of the waitresses.

Although Ken lived literally across the road, we wouldn't be walking. Nobody walked anywhere out here. Besides, once past the first set of electric gates, we would be in lion country. Jack lowered his window and pressed the intercom button and spoke briefly. Moments later the huge metal gates slid open. As we drove through they closed behind us. Across a wooden bridge we eventually reached a twelve foot high security fence and another intercom on a post. Again Jack pressed the button and spoke and the gates slid open. As we pulled up outside a very impressive house, Ken emerged with two adult male lions.

'Jeeesus!' Was all that Em could manage to say. As we got out of the truck she stayed very close to me.

'Don't be shy, come and meet Tyson and Inca.' Said Ken. He was holding them by their manes, presumably to stop them bounding towards us to say hello.

'Shit Ken, Tyson's grown a bit hasn't he?'

'Yep. He's a big lad now.' I'd rolled around playing with him on Ken's lounge floor when he was about six months old. I didn't fancy doing that again in a hurry.

Tyson had other ideas. As I got close to him he stood on his hind legs and plonking a paw on each of my shoulders he licked me from chin to forehead. I rubbed his belly for him.

'Hello my boy. Do you remember me eh? Good boy Tyson. Good boy!' 'Yea good boy, don't eat me.' Is what I meant. When he eventually got down Inca, probably thinking 'Any mate of Tyson's is a mate of mine' took his place on my shoulders.

'If I get burgled I'll know who it was.' Laughed Ken. 'These are my guard dogs. Nobody would dare come onto my property uninvited.'

'That's a point. Where are your dogs Ken?'

'Both dead, I'm afraid. Alfie died of old age. He was 14 bless him. Rex, the German shepherd was unfortunately killed by Tyson. Nothing nasty. No they were playing and Tyson just gave him a swat. You know how cats kind of swat with their front paws? Well he doesn't know his own strength. He snapped Rex's neck. I saw it happen.' Ken clicked his fingers. 'Just like that.I can't get any more dogs now. These two were fine with Alfie and Rex 'cause they grew up with them. They were part of the family. I wouldn't be able to introduce a new dog now. They wouldn't tolerate it. No these two are my guard dogs now.'

'As long as you don't get the same shit Ed had a few years back.' Jack said what I'd been thinking.

There had been a bungled robbery attempt at the ticket office at the Rhino reserve. Three armed black men had burst in there just before the park was due to close. Their first mistake was that the money had already been collected and was in the safe in the main office. Things went from bad to worse. They ran out to their getaway car which wouldn't start. Meanwhile the guy in the ticket office radioed for help. Land rovers full of armed rangers began to arrive. Two of the robbers had surrendered. The third decided to leg it. He ran across the road and scaling a fence found himself in a compound with Ed's pair of Bengalese tigers. How's that for karma? Believe it or not, the dead man's parents sued Ed. They'd obviously watched too much American TV. Unbelievably they won, because Ed hadn't displayed any warning signs.

'Ah.' Said Ken. 'I have signs in English, Tswana, Zulu, Afrikaans, Xhosa, Swazi, Tsonga, Venda, Ndebele, Northern Sotho, Sotho and frigging Braille! I've got a good lawyer. My ass is covered. I've even got pictures in case the thieving gits can't read.'

Chapter seventy two

We spent the next hour having a guided tour of all the various compounds housing Ken's 'puddy-tats.' He'd rescued them from all over Africa for one reason or another. The cost must've been enormous. Transportation, their enclosures, food and vet fees. Ken was obviously not short of a few bob. When we went in to see his cheetah I helped distract Dune, the male while Ken clipped his claws. He explained that he wasn't actually clipping them. He was just going through the motions. He was busy cursing his ex-wife as he battled with the cat. He told us that cheetah can't retract their claws, in that respect they were more like a dog than a cat. It was vital to trim them regularly or even playing could result in some nasty cuts, concidering you were usually wearing shorts and t-shirt. By clipping their nails on a daily basis from a young age the cats just got used to it. As he'd said, even if they didn't need clipping you still had to go through the motions. His ex-wife had let the routine slip and consequently Ken was now having to 'teach an old dog new tricks.' Amber, the female was much more amenable, lying on her back, legs akimbo for Ken to snip away. These two were part of a captive breeding programme.

Contrary to popular belief the rarest big cat in Africa is not the leopard. It is in fact the cheetah.

Ken explained that it was a common misconception that the leopard was thought to be the rarest. 'Just because they're rarely seen doesn't mean they're not there! Ok one last job to do then we'll go and get a drink in my bar.'

That one last job involved Ken going into a compound with three adult lion and rubbing ointment on the ears of two of them.

'That bugger over there keeps chewing the ears on these two. If I don't keep putting this on them they'll get infected.' Said Ken.

Everyone locally knew that one of these days he would be killed by his cats. He probably knew it himself. Nice bloke, but an absolute nutter!

Ken had a bar alright! It was a converted mill. Inside was a huge bar complete with cinema and surround sound. Outside was being converted into a trout farm. Very impressive. After a couple of beers I asked Ken where the loos were. He said that they weren't built yet and I'd have to go over to the house. I asked him where Inca and Tyson were.

'Oh they'll be out there somewhere.'

I decided I could wait for a pee until we got back to Jack's!

Chapter seventy three

Back at the lodge I made a bee-line for the loo, while Em went to check on Charlie.

He was fast asleep on Precious's back. She'd strapped him to her using a towel, and was wandering around the dining room putting out crockery and cutlery as if he wasn't even there. When she saw Em she 'shooed' her away with a smile. We got changed and went out to the pool and lounged around. About an hour later Charlie woke up and Precious brought him out to us. 'I did feed him some cereal and he's had some pap. He likes it Miss Emma. I think something is happening in his trousers.' She said holding her nose.

'Thank you Precious.' I said slipping her ten bucks. Her eyes lit up and she thanked me.

'What's pap?' Asked Em.

'It's mealie-meal. A bit like porridge. It's their staple diet out here. Tastes bleeding awful if you ask me.'

While Em took Charlie back to the room to change his nappy and bath him I sat at the bar chatting with Jack. At just after 5pm the rangers from the Rhino Reserve began drifting in. It was the norm for them to pop in for a beer on their way home.

My man had kept his word and had brought with him a selection of hand guns for me to look at. I went with him to his 'backie' to check them over. He had a Berretta PX4, a gen4 Glock 17 and a Springfield XDM. I liked the look and feel of the XDM. I hadn't fired one but had heard good things about it. Apparently it was becoming the weapon of choice of more and more US cops.
I liked the fact that it had a 19 round mag. I was torn between it and the Glock. Sensing my dilemma he said 'Don't choose now. Come over to the reserve tomorrow. Bring the wife and kid. They can play with the animals and we can go to the range and fire off some rounds.'
'Ok.' I said 'You're on. Now come back inside so I can buy you a beer. By the way, how do you pronounce your name?'
'Vynandt.'
'Cool. Lets have a beer Vynnn.Vine, Vinny. Mate.'
We went back inside and I saw Em. She was talking to Lils. They were sat with another couple of people I vaguely remembered seeing before. I got myself and Vinny a beer, miming in Em's direction 'drink?' They all mimed back 'no'. After firming up a time to go to the Rhino Reserve, I made my way over to them.
'This is Jan and Chloe. They're the people that need house-sitters. I recommended you and Em.' Said Lils. Anyway, over the course

of a few beers we ironed out the 'contract'. Basically, what it boiled down to was that we would be staying on their small holding, a few miles up the road for 3 weeks, starting at the weekend. We just had to be there and feed the dogs. In return we could eat and drink whatever we liked. It seemed a good deal to me. Free board and lodgings plus we wouldn't be infringing on Jack and Karen's hospitality for too long.

At the bar I had a chat with Jack. I wanted to take Em and Charlie to Sun City for a few days. With the house-sitting coming up at the week-end it meant we'd either have to go the next day, or go in three weeks time. I rang the booking office and reserved a family room at The Palace for three nights. Last of the big spenders me. Jack said he would lend us a car, and tomorrow, would show us on the map the best way to go. Em came and sat at the bar with us. 'What are you two plotting?' She asked me.

'Ah now that would be telling.'

'Come on Charlie, stop teasing.'

'Ok. You need to pack a bag. We're going to Sun City for a few days. We'll be going tomorrow afternoon and coming back on Saturday to do the house-sitting thing.'

'Sun City's that place you told me about? A bit like Las Vegas yeh?'

'That's the one. It was built for the same reason, gambling. It's an amazing place. Nice hotels and restaurants. When I say nice I mean fantastic. Whacko Jacko used to stay here regularly. I almost got run over by him in a golf buggy his kid was driving. True. There's even a man made beach, complete with wave machine. There's a log ride that goes right round the whole beach area. Charlie will love that.'

'Sounds great. I can't wait.'

'Before all that I've got another little treat for you both. Tomorrow morning we're going to the Rhino Park and you and Charlie get to play with white lion cubs.'

Chapter seventy four

Over breakfast Jack said he could spare a few hours to take us to the Rhino park. He said it would be easier as he knew his way round the park and it would save us getting lost.

Fed and watered we all got into his truck and he drove the 2km to the park gates. The guy on the cash desk had obviously been told that we were coming, as he waved us through.

We drove slowly through the reserve with Jack pointing out the various critters that we passed. We saw zebra, kudu, impala, wildebeest and buffalo, one of the 'big five.'

When we arrived at the restaurant and petting area, 'Vinny' was waiting for me. I left Em and Charlie with Jack and jumped in the land rover with the ranger. We drove out to the middle of nowhere, where the rangers had set up a makeshift range. We put on ear-defenders and I blatted off a few mags-worth of rounds with each of the three hand guns that Vinney had brought for me to sample. They were all pretty good but I found myself leaning towards the Springfield XDM. After firing off a few more mags, I stripped the weapon down and re-assembled it. It was a nice compact weapon and I liked it. It was more than accurate enough, and shit, with 19 rounds per mag, you ought to be able to hit what you were aiming at. I settled on a price and payed him.

I got a pleasant surprise back in the vehicle when Vinny gave me the purpose built case and accessories kit that came with the handgun. It was as good as new. I was a happy bunny.

So apparently was Em. She was grinning from ear to ear when I met back up with her and Charlie at the petting zoo. Charlie was sat on the ground with half a dozen tiny lion cubs climbing all over him. Em was clicking away like mad with her camera.

Half an hour later I managed to drag them away. 'Come on we've got some travelling to do. Don't worry we'll come back again. Tell you what, when we do, you won't believe how much those cubs will have grown.' As I waited for them to get their stuff together I transferred my XDM from Vinny's land rover to Jack's truck.

Back at Jack's we grabbed a quick bite to eat and he talked me through the journey to Sun City. He showed me on the map. There were several ways to go, but I decided on the 'scenic' route, via Hartbeespoort dam. The journey would take about an hour and a half.

If we left soon we'd be at Sun City long before dark. The last 50km or so of the drive was on a very dodgy stretch of road. Cattle and other livestock in the road being the hazard, as opposed to car-jacking or any other human danger.

It was a fast stretch of road with no fencing and no lighting.

We got our baggage out to the truck. Not having a child seat Em sat in the back with Charlie. A quick stop in Muldersdrif for fuel and 'nibbles' for the trip, and we were off.

Chapter seventy five

We had a pleasant journey. The scenery was spectacular, especially around Hartbeespoort dam. The road followed most of the way around the huge dam and then eventually crossed it. The roads were all well sign-posted and that, along with the fact I had travelled the route before, meant we got to Sun City without any dramas.

There are four hotels plus a time-share set up at Sun City. We were booked into the best hotel, The Palace. We got the VIP treatment from the minute we pulled into the underground car park. The last time I had stayed at Sun City Michael Jackson had rented most of one floor of the Palace. It was, and may still be, rated in the top ten hotels in the world. Stunning and extravagant are just a few words you could use to describe the hotel. Well the whole of the complex really. I could tell that Em was totally awestruck.

We had a fabulous stay at the Palace, at Sun City in general. We even got to see Michael Buble at the Sun Superbowl. Charlie loved swimming in the hotel pool but especially loved the 'Valley of the waves.' We won a few bucks on the slots and lost it all back at the roulette table!

Black Heart

All in all we had a great time.

When we arrived back at Jack's it was back to earth with a bump.

I'd had an unwelcome visitor.

Chapter seventy six

As we pulled into the car park at the back of Kenjara, Precious came running towards the car from her room, 'Mr Jack is resting so please go around the front way to your room so you do not wake him. Also a man came here just now. He was asking for you Mr Charlie. I told him you were not staying here, like Mr Jack ask me to say. He did not believe me Mr Charlie. He gave to me this paper and told me to give it to you. Here, I am giving it to you.'
'Thank you Precious.Don't worry, you did a good job. When Mr Jack wakes up, tell him I will bring his truck back later. Ok?' I passed her ten bucks and got back in the truck. As I drove around to the front of the lodge I unfolded the piece of paper.One word 'Peregrine'.And a phone number. I didn't need that piece of information. I knew the number off-by-heart.
We got the rest of our belongings from our room. As Em changed Charlie's nappy I txt 'Falcon' to Dimitri.Thirty seconds later he phoned me.
'Dimitri, what took you so long?'
'Hey Charlie.Don't worry we knew you were in SA from the time you used your credit card to alter your flight details. 'Big Brother'again. 'So why wait until now to get in touch?'

Black Heart

'Come on Charlie, Africa is quite a big place. We did our best.'
'I take it you want to meet, you're in Jo'berg?'
'How did you know that? Yes, I want to meet you. I have something important to talk about.' It was a lucky guess about Jo'berg; still keep him on his toes, eh?
'Ok come to 'Carnivors' Anyone will tell you where it is, I'll book a table for 7.30pm. Make sure you're hungry, you'll need to be.' I hung up.

Em and Charlie got in the truck and we drove the couple of miles up the road to our house-sitting job. After a quick tour of the house and surroundings, what food to give what dog etc, Jan and Chloe set off on their vacation, leaving us in charge of their worldly goods.It was quite a nice place. All mod-cons, satellite TV, well stocked fridge and larder. More importantly, a very well stocked wine cellar and bar. Oh, and they had a swimming pool and a hot tub.

As Em was about to do dinner I told her I had to take Jack's truck back. 'Don't worry about me. I'll get something to eat at his while I'm waiting for a lift back.' I gave her a kiss and headed off to my meeting with Dimitri.

Chapter seventy seven

As I walked into 'Carnivors' I could see Dimitri waiting at the bar, sipping on a small beer. I ordered myself a beer and we were shown to our table. We did nothing but exchange pleasantries until the fourth or fifth course. So far we'd sampled chicken, beef, lamb, impala and crocodile. And maybe something else. It's hard to tell at this restaurant, food just keeps coming.

I broke the ice. 'So Dimitri, why are you here? I know about 'The Accountant', the $500million. Why you didn't want a body to be found. I did what you wanted. So, I repeat, why are you here?'

'The original plan was to take him out. No body. However, nothing gets past our current administration. There is now a new plan. Obama and his people see this as a 'double whammy'. They don't just want to freeze their assets and stop their man running for president. They want to confiscate their 'ill-gotten-gains' and use them to fund the fight against organised crime. Big vote winner that.'

'Clever move, I have to say. However, back to my original question. Why are you here?'

'We now believe Czeckov had the money stashed in hundreds of off-shore accounts, the details of which are all stored on his smart-phone.'

Black Heart

'Can I stop you there? You want his phone right?' I'd decided to tease him.
'Yes, that's right.'
'But that wasn't the deal Dimitri. You payed me to make him disappear I did. You never mentioned his phone.'
'So you don't have it?'
'I didn't say that Dimitri.' Another course of food arrived. Springbok, I think.
'So you do have it?'
'I didn't say that either. How's your food?'
'Charlie. Stop playing games. Do you have Czeckov's phone or not?' I now knew that my friend Dimitri had been acting 'unofficially' when he'd asked me to kill Czeckov. If he'd been 'legit' he wouldn't be here. He'd know where the phone was. He'd been working for Red.
I tried a piece of the latest meat to arrive on my plate. It was nice, it was indeed Springbok, and unsurprisingly, tasted like venison. I took a swig of wine and then continued 'playing games.' as Dimitri had put it.
'Ok Dimitri. As I see it the plans have changed. You're no longer 'freezing' the baddie's money so that they can't use it to fund their campaign. You're now going after their cash.'
'Well yes we . . .'

'So the way I see it, the 'vanished for a year' deal is no longer relevant, right?'

'Well . . .'

'In other words, if I tell you where Czeckov's phone is, you can pay me my balance. Call it a 'finder's fee.' After all, if my maths is correct it amounts to 0.1%. Well actually slightly more, as we're talking £500.000 out of $500, 000, 000.'

He sat for a moment, then rose saying 'I'm going to the rest room I will make a call.'

While he was gone I also made a call.

'Jack, Charlie. How much do you trust me? That off-shore account of yours, can I have the number?' He hesitated. 'I need to have a large sum of money paid in there. I will pay you 10% handling fee.'

'How much are we talking?'

'Your cut, depending on the exchange rate, will be about half a million rand.' Sounded better in rand. He gave me the number and I wrote it on a napkin.

Dimitri arrived at the same time as another course of meat, zebra this time.

'Jesus! When does the food stop coming in this place?'

Black Heart

'I told you to make sure you were hungry. The meat just keeps coming until you surrender.' He looked puzzled so I explained that the way it worked at Carnivors is that the food kept coming until you displayed the white flag on your table.Signalling your surrender.

'The office agreed your terms. So where is the phone?' I passed him the napkin.

'When the money clears in that account I'll contact you.'

We surrendered.

Chapter seventy eight

I waited for Dimitri to drive off before I headed back to Kenjara. I stopped on the way to check if I was being followed. The beauty of dirt roads in the middle of nowhere is that it's pretty easy to spot another vehicle.Unless of course the vehicle didn't have lights on. I drove as fast as was safe with my lights on. No way could anyone follow at that speed without lights. I stopped at Jack's for a beer and explained about the payment that was due to appear in his account. Obviously I made up a story; I didn't tell him it was payment for a contract killing! I told him it was from a house sale that I didn't want to pay tax on.

I phoned Em to check that everything was ok on the house-sitting front. I said I would be back soon and to get the dogs in so that they didn't maul me when I returned.

'Do you need your truck back tonight Jack, or can I drop it off for you tomorrow?'

'Yea yeh no prob's.Are you off then?'

'Have to really mate, Em's on her own in a strange place. Don't want her to panic, it is a bit remote out on Jan's farm. I'll see you tomorrow, and thanks for the bank thing. I could do with you showing me how to set up an account. Also, don't forget I'm still

Black Heart

looking for a truck.I'm sorted 'til Jan gets back, so I've got three weeks to find one.'

'Word's out on the truck and we'll sort the account out tomorrow. Get yourself back and protect that little lady and kid of yours.' He liked Em. It was easy to tell with Jack.

'Little lady.' That's not what I found when I got back to the farm. Horny blonde chick, stark-naked in the hot tub with a bottle of wine and two glasses is what I found!

Chapter seventy nine

I was almost asleep when my phone beeped. I looked at the message. It was Dimitri. Getting out of bed I sent the usual response. No point waking everyone up, so I stood out by the pool waiting for the call. I looked at my watch it was 11.40pm. When the call came it was brief.

'Check your account and ring me back.' That was it. I was fairly sure Jack wouldn't be asleep yet. The bar was probably still open. On quiet nights he did close early, but it had seemed fairly busy when I'd left. I phoned him. He was about to close for the night. I asked him to check his account and ring me back. I had a sudden need for a cigarette. I bet I hadn't smoked half a dozen since we got to SA, but I needed one now.

I sat smoking my fag in the silence.Except it wasn't silent. It was the silence of an African night, crickets clicking, frogs croaking and the occasional roar from a lion. We were up on a hill and in the distance I could see the lights of Jo'berg. I liked this place. When Jan got back from his holidays I might just make him an offer. My phone rang. It was Jack. He was happy. The £400k was in his account.

'You know Charlie, for a couple of grand I could have you killed and keep the lot.'

'Yeh, thanks for that sobering thought mate. I'll see you tomorrow.'

Now for the tricky bit. I was about to discover, once and for all, what Dimitri was really up to. One phone call should confirm my suspicions about him. If he was 'legit' and for some reason wasn't aware of the phones location, the fact that my office had it and were working on the coded accounts would be great news. His people could liaise with mine and work to a common end. No skin off his nose, after all it wasn't his money he'd just paid me. If, on the other hand, he wasn't 'legit,' well the shit was about to hit the fan!

I rang him and told him where the phone was.

Before going in to bed I got my XDM from under the seat in Jack's truck.

I lit another fag then made another call, to my boss.

This was the first time I'd ever phoned my boss at home. At least it wasn't too late, the UK being an hour behind SA time. I had a distinct feeling that if I was right about Dimitri he would come after me. Not personally, he would send the 'hired help.' I just wanted to make sure that, if anything did happen to me, that I'd at least 'marked his card.'

I could tell my boss was glad to hear from me. I could also tell that I was in a bit of shit, for 'doing one.' When I'd pointed out that I was on leave he treated that comment with the respect it deserved. Not. I told him that I intended to resign and would send that wish in writing. I then went on to tell him everything I knew about Czeckov, using the correct phone protocol and obviously not being too openly specific about naming names etc. I also missed out the bit about me being the killer.

I finished the conversation by telling him that 'D' either was Red, or if not was definitely working for him, and that I thought he might be targeting me. My boss tried several times to talk me into coming back and sorting things out but I kept refusing. When I hung up I knew I'd burnt some bridges.

I also knew that if Dimitri was going to do anything, he'd do it sooner rather than later.

I slept with one eye open that night.My pistol under my pillow.

Chapter eighty

I didn't sleep very well. I'd slept for an hour then woken up, slept an hour, woke up. I remember Em getting up in the night to see to Charlie. She was now back in bed fast asleep. I'd been woken up this time by a distant buzzing, whining noise. I couldn't work out what it was, but I was awake now so I got up. I made a cup of black coffee and sat outside by the pool drinking it. Ten minutes or so later Em came and joined me.

'Morning. No Charlie?' I asked her.

'No, he's still sleeping. Kettle's on, do you want another?'

'Yeh, cheers.' I passed her my empty cup and she returned a few minutes later with a re-fill for me and a cup of tea for herself.

'Any plans for today Charlie?'

'Not really. I've got to take Jack's truck back, but it's too early now, he won't be up yet. Apart from that I have no plans.'

'Do you need me to follow you in Jan's truck to give you a lift back?'

'No ta. I'll jog back, it's not far. Besides, I could do with some exercise, I've done bugger all since we arrived.'

'I think you've been very athletic. I could give you a bit more exercise now if you like? After all, little Charlie's asleep.'

An hour or so later I escaped from the bedroom and dived into the pool.
After a few lengths I showered and dressed in shorts, t-shirt and trainers. I dug my small rucksack from my luggage and put the XDM along with a spare mag inside. I grabbed a bottle of water from the fridge and put that in aswell. Kissing Em and Charlie good bye, I got in Jack's truck and drove the 3 or 4kms to Kenjara Lodge. As I drove up his driveway I noticed something odd.
 Behind his property, way up on top of a mountain, in between half a dozen aerial masts, something was glinting in the sunlight. I pulled up round the back, near the kitchen door, which was open. As I got out of the truck I could just see the strange glint above the single storey building. I ducked. Just in time as a puff of sandy soil erupted directly behind me.

Chapter eighty one

Jack, who was now stood at the kitchen door, hadn't seen or heard a thing. Keeping my head down I went into the kitchen.
'Stiff back or something?' Jack asked. I nearly was a 'stiff' I thought. I carried on through the kitchen, into the dining room, Jack following in my wake. Keeping way back from the windows I stared up at the mountain. The glint of light was still there. What I was looking at was the sunlight reflecting off the lens of a telescopic sight, attached to a silenced high power sniper rifle.
'Keep back from the windows Jack. Do you have a pair of binoculars I can borrow?'
'Yes, but what's happening Charlie?'
'That glint of light up there is the reflection from a sniper's rifle. Get me the bins Jack. Quick as you can mate.' When he returned with them he said. 'No doubt this is connected with the cash in my account. I thought that was too good to be true.'
I ignored him and considered my options. I couldn't make a move towards the mountain and I couldn't drive off. Maybe under cover of darkness, but it wouldn't be dark for another 7hrs or so. We were trapped.

Bringing the bins up to my eyes I asked him how you got up the mountain. I couldn't see the sniper and the glint was no longer there.

'You can't see it from here, but there's a track on the other side. I walked it once, a long time ago. It's bloody steep.'

'Could you drive up there?'

'No chance, you would'nt even get a four-wheel-drive up there.'

Maybe not I thought as the buzzing, whining sound started up in the distance.The same noise that had woken me this morning. But you could obviously get up there on a trials bike, or scrambler.

A nasty thought occurred to me. From his vantage point up there, the sniper had almost certainly seen my entire journey. He obviously hadn't known about Jan's place when he got into position. He had set up and waited for me to show my face at Kenjara, which is obviously where he'd expected me to be. He hadn't known where I was actually staying.

 He certainly did now.

I rang Em. No answer. She could be swimming, feeding Charlie, having a shower. God knows.

'Come Jack. We're out of his line of vision while he's going down the other side of that mountain. I need you to drop me at Jan's. I need to get Em and Charlie out of there'.

Chapter eighty two

Jack drove as quickly as he dared on the dirt road. I tried ringing Em again. This time she answered. I told her to grab some things, nappies etc. and find Jan's keys and start up his truck. I'd be with her in a few minutes.

I could see a dust trail heading diagonally across country from Jack's. He was quite a way behind us but would soon be able to pick up speed once on the dirt road. We hung a right into Jan's drive. I jumped out and opened the gate. Jack pulled through and I re-shut the gate. Up at the house Em was just locking up. She had a bag full of 'Charlie-stuff' and was holding the keys to Jan's truck. I took them from her and started the vehicle. I told Jack he'd be fine. The biker would certainly follow me. Then I had an idea. 'Can you leave after us? Shut the gate mate to keep the dogs in.' I told Em to strap in tight and I floored it, back towards Kenjara. The dust still hadn't settled from our journey to Jan's but I could just make out the motorcyclist hurtling towards us. At the last second I turned the wheel and hit him head-on.

He was launched over the truck, his bike cart-wheeling into a ditch. Em screamed. I turned the truck around and drove back to where the sniper lay. I told Em to sit tight and I got out and checked the body for a pulse. He was dead. He hadn't been wearing a helmet so his face was a bit of a mess. Even so I recognised him. The last time I'd seen him he was wearing a dark suit and was sat at the bar in The Barbican Hotel, waiting to have dinner with Vladimir Czeckov.

Black Heart

Jack pulled up alongside me and got out. 'Dead?'

'Yep. What do we do now?'

'You get going. Leave this to me. It's a dangerous road and he wasn't wearing a helmet. Accidents happen. I know the local cops; they all drink in my bar. I'll ring them and tell them I just came across a hit-and-run. Get going I'll talk to you later.'

I unstrapped the rifle from the side of the bike and, checking the body I found his phone. Putting both in Jan's truck I drove to Muldersdrif. I pulled into the car park of a roadside bar and ordered two brandies, two beers and an orange juice.

Chapter eighty three

'Here, neck this.' I handed Em a brandy and downed mine in one. Em drank the brandy. She sipped it though, rather than knocking it back in one.

'Charlie I thought we'd left all that shit behind us. That man back there, on the motor bike, that was no accident. You hit him. Deliberately.Charlie please.Tell me what's going on. Charlie?'

I held her hand across the table. I decided to tell her the truth. Well, some of it.

'Em, I also thought we'd left all the shit, as you put it, behind us. That man tried to shoot me. You saw the rifle that was strapped to his motorbike.He knew where we live. He wouldn't stop until he shot me. Any witnesses, ie you and Charlie, Jack aswell, would also have been shot. I really had no choice. I had to stop him. You understand that don't you?'

'But where does it end? Why did he want to shoot you? Who was he?'

'It's all linked to the two Russians that payed you a visit. I had to find out who my friends are.I found out. I've got one more little trick up my sleeve. If it works we'll be sorted.'

'And if it doesn't Charlie? What then?'

I didn't want to contemplate failure. It would mean getting the office involved. Going back to the UK and facing the music. No I didn't like that option.

'This will work Em. Two phone calls and it will be sorted. Trust me, I'm a doctor.'

I went out to the truck and got the sniper's cell-phone. I turned it on, (I'd turned it off earlier) I went to the call register. The last few calls had been to and from Dimitri. No shocks there. The log told a story. The previous night, two minutes after I'd phoned Dimitri to give him the location of Czechov's mobile; he'd placed a 3 minute call to my friend the sniper. This morning the sniper had made a 27 second call to Dimitri, presumeably to tell him that he was in position.

I took out my phone and rang Dimitri. I wasn't surprised when he didn't answer. I waited for the answerphone to kick in. When it did I sang into the phone 'In the jungle, the mighty jungle . . .' I hung up.

A few minutes later the sniper's phone rang. I accepted the call and in my finest baritone sang 'The lion sleeps tonight.' The line went dead.

Right.I'd sent Dimitri a message. As I saw it he had two options. He would either get the fuck out of here on the first available flight. Or he would come looking for me.

We popped into the supermarket for milk and a few other bits and pieces, and then I drove us back to the farm. I'd thought about booking Em and Charlie into a hotel or guest house.

I decided against that idea. Dimitri could ring round or even visit them all.There were only a handful in the area. No, the farm was the safest place. I tried to put myself in Dimitri's shoes.He wouldn't get on a flight out of here. He would definitely want me dead. For revenge.But also, because I could testify against him. I knew too much. Even though he knew I probably wouldn't be at Kenjara, where else could he start the search for me? He wouldn't have sent the sniper to Jack's if he'd known about the farm. The more I thought about it the more I was sure that the farm was the safest place for Em and Charlie to be.

I made a few calls. First I rang Jack to see how things had gone. It was all sorted. I said I'd see him later. Next I rang Lils. I told her that I had to go away for the night and asked if she would stop at the farm to keep Em company.The mention of a bottle of 'Spiced Gold' made that a no-brainer for her.

Finally I rang Vinny. I asked if he had some night-vision bins or a rifle with a night-vision 'scope that he could lend to me.
He had both. Top man.
I arranged to meet him at Kenjara just after 5pm.
I showered and changed into black jeans and t-shirt. I laced up my boots. I swapped the XDM spare mag and water to my larger back pack, adding some warm clothing. It could get bloody cold out there at night, especially if I had to lie around waiting for Dimitri to show.
I gave Em a hug. She wasn't too keen on me going out for the night. I told her that Lils would be over soon and warned her not to try and keep up with her in the drinking department. I told her that I'd rung the man behind all the shit, her words. I said that if he didn't show up tonight then he wasn't going to in future. Besides, if he had any sense he'd be on a flight to Moscow. I kissed her goodbye and left the house. As I got into Jan's truck I marvelled at the slight 'ding' in the bull-bars, the only sign of the earlier 'accident.'
As I pulled into Jack's drive I turned my phone onto 'silent.'

Chapter eighty four

I parked the truck so that I could leave in a hurry if necessary. Vinny and two other rangers were sat together at the corner of the bar. I went over to them and got them all a drink. I ordered myself a coke. I went out to the car park with Vinny and transferred the night vision gear into Jan's truck. I bunged him 1000 rand.I asked him if he'd like to double that, and if he thought one of his workmates might want to earn a grand aswell.

'What do you need Charlie? Johan, the guy sitting next to me is a good bloke.'

'I'm expecting an unwelcome guest. You guys know this area. You could spot a strange vehicle straight away. I'm fairly sure the vehicle will be coming here, around or just after dark It will be coming from Jo'berg.and will almost definitely be a hire car (hire cars were easy to spot in SA as they had different coloured registration plates), and I think, no hope, there will be one male driver on board. Do you reckon you guys can position yourselves a few miles away, and when you spot it, give me a call on my mobile to let me know?'

'That's it? You don't want his tyres shooting out or anything'

'Thanks for the offer Vinny. No, I just need to know when he's here. You've got my phone number? Make sure Johan has it too.'

'You'll need to go and get into your positions soon. I'm going to go and make myself part of the scenery across the road there.'

I went to Jan's truck and grabbed my kit. In the back of the truck I found some useful items, an axe a roll of wire and some pliers. I had quite a lot to carry so I had a change of plan. I drove down the drive and turned right onto the dirt road. A few metres up the road I stopped and unloaded all my kit into a ditch. I then turned the truck around and took it back to the car park at Jack's.

I jogged back to my cache. I moved everything into cover and then took the rifles and night vision bins a few hundred yards into the bush.

They would be of no use close to the road anyway. Car headlights would cause all sorts of problems. I checked the XDM and loaded it. Undoing my belt I attached the spare mag clip and holster and then loading the spare mag and holstering the pistol I re-buckled my belt. I still had a few hours of daylight so I used the time to set a few 'booby-traps.'

I sharpened half a dozen wooden stakes and embedded them in the ditch at the side of the road.

Above them I built a dummy bridge, consisting of a couple of poles, and a false walkway. This was made of reeds. In the dark it would just look like a simple bridge across a ditch.

One step onto it and you would find it wasn't a bridge at all. Bosh. Belly-flop onto a bunch of wooden stakes.

I saw Vinny and Johan set off a few minutes apart to do look-out duty. Occasionally a passing vehicle caused me to take cover in the bushes. Luckily this was not a particularly busy road, so I didn't have too many interruptions.

 I made a few spring traps out of bent down saplings, pegged, with wire nooses. I also strung a few wires at ankle level at intervals throughout the cover and embedded sharpened wooden stakes in front of them.

There wasn't a lot I could do now but wait. I was pretty sure he would come. If he did it would be around dark. He was 100% certain to come through Muldersdrif which meant he would approach from my left from where I was now, sat in the bushes opposite Kenjara lodge. I sat and visualised what would happen. No. I was in the wrong place. I crossed the ditch, then the dirt road and settled down with my back to a tree in Jack's driveway. When Dimitri approached the lodge he would swing left into the driveway. His headlights would pass over me as he turned in. He would get a good, but brief look at me. I would then leg it across the road and into the ditch. It would take him a moment or two to get out of the car and give chase.

Black Heart

I would make sure he got a brief glimpse of me disappearing into the bushes, and hey presto, he was in my domain. I would now hold all the aces.

That was the theory anyway. I lit a cigarette and sat back to wait. He would come, wouldn't he? Part of me hoped he would just get on a plane and piss off. On the other hand, this confrontation would happen, sooner or later. Better sooner. At least now it would be under my control. Well I did have home advantage.

As I sat there in the dark, leaning against a tree, two things happened.

The lions began to roar, and my phone vibrated in my pocket.

Chapter eighty five

The news from Vinny was not what I'd wanted to hear. A hire car with a male driver and three male passengers was about 6kms from me, heading my way. He said he'd not seen the vehicle before and it was definitely not from around here on account of how clean it was. It had definitely not been on any dirt roads, until now. I told him to stay put, just in case this turned out to be a false alarm. I lit a cig. I had at least 5 or 6 minutes until it got Here. If indeed it was heading here. A feeling in my guts told me that it was.

By the time I'd finished my smoke I could see headlights approaching. About 500mtrs away the car stopped. I distinctly heard two doors close. At least two of them had got out of the car. Was that good or bad? Well four onto one is not good odds. Two lots of two onto one is better. Except of course I didn't know where the other two were. I assumed that they'd been dropped off so that they could make their way around the back of Jack's place.

The car was on the move again. I stood in the shadows and waited. When the car turned into the drive I made my move. As the headlights turned across me I legged it past the car, across the road and into the ditch. As I'd passed the car I'd seen Dimitri at the wheel, another man in the front passenger seat. Two lots of two it was then. Dimitri didn't stop the car. Instead he reversed back out of the drive at break-neck speed, hung a hard left and ended up, virtually parked at the side of the road. The headlights were on me as I ducked into cover about level with my 'bridge.' The lights went out, doors slammed and I heard the sound of them running after me. I stopped, just inside the deep cover and waited, pistol drawn. One of them hit the 'bridge' running. A sickeningly squelchy thud followed by 'Aaargh.' meant one down, three to go. Whichever one hadn't just been impaled hesitated the other side of the ditch. Meanwhile I could hear two people running flat out from the other direction. Come to daddy, I thought as I made my way deeper into the thick cover.

Chapter eighty six

I was fairly certain that Dimitri would've sent the hired help in after me first.In which case it hadn't been him that was now impaled in the ditch. From what I knew about him he'd had no military training. I was sure he could handle a weapon, but aiming at a target on a nice warm, well lit range, would not have prepared him for the situation he now found himself in. The other two men didn't appear to be brimming over with field craft either, judging by the way they were crashing through the undergrowth. It was only a matter of time before. As I thought it one of them triggered one of my booby-traps.He'd run into a trip wire and would now be wearing a very sharp wooden stake, depending on his height, somewhere between his groin and stomach. Two down, two to go. Importantly, so far no shots fired either. I was fairly sure that the odd shot fired wouldn't draw too much attention. A full on fire fight would be a different matter.

Over to my left I could hear the remaining guy moving a lot more cautiously than before.

I had heard nothing from Dimitri's direction. Had he chickened out and legged it? I made my way slowly over to where I'd stashed the night-vision bins. Over to my left I could see the guy, crouched beside a tree. I scanned the whole area in front and to my right, but there was no sign of Dimitri. I picked up the rifle and with the cross-hairs steadily on the other guy's forehead, I squeezed off a single round. He fell backwards, dead. Shit that was loud. The rifle also had a hell of a kick. I'd thought it would have and had allowed for it when I'd fired. I scanned front and right again.Nothing. Where the hell was Dimitri?

Two or three minutes passed. I stayed perfectly still and listened. Way over to my left I heard a twig snap. I turned the rifle. Had I missed the last guy? No it was a definite hit. Maybe the first guy had only been injured, and not killed by the stake. Or had Dimitri Made his way up the dirt road and come in from my left? I saw a figure move. I gently began to apply pressure on the trigger. Come on. Step out from behind that bush. One more step. Bingo. Gotcha!

Chapter eighty seven

Luckily for him I had a perfect view of him, so hadn't fired. It vas Vinny. What a prat.

I was sure he was trying to help but he'd nearly died trying. I watched him lean forward at roughly the spot where I'd dropped the last guy. He stood again and began to approach me. I could see him stepping very carefully, scanning left and right, his 9mm held out in front of him in a double-handed grip. His job as a game ranger had taught him stealth. It was quite impressive to watch him approach. If I was marking him out of ten, I'd probably give him a nine. Having said that, if I was the enemy he'd be 'brown bread' now. When he was within a few feet I said 'Pssst Vinney. Down.' He quickly knelt down beside me.

'Shit Charlie, you made me jump.'

'What are you doing here? I almost shot you.' I whispered.

'Sorry but four onto one didn't seem fair odds to me. Obviously I underestimated you. Did you get all of them?'

'No the boss man is still out here somewhere. I haven't seen him at all, not since he reversed his car and I ran into this cover. He has to be over there to our right. Mate you need to stay out of this. Thanks for your offer but I can do this on my own. I might need some help to get rid of the bodies though. Where's your truck?'
'Back up the road there.'
'Ok. Go and get it. Go this way, and watch out for traps, there are still a few left and right. Go straight ahead and you'll be fine.'
As he moved forward I went to the right. After I'd gone about 50metres I stopped and listened.Nothing. Then I had an idea. I took out my cell-phone and rang Dimitri.
About 20 seconds later his phone rang. It rang several times before he could silence it.
Gotcha! He hadn't legged it. The crafty bugger was way over to my right. He'd flanked me. I made my way as quickly and quietly as I could in his direction. When I got to the high fence I realised where I was. I could hear him running up ahead of me. I climbed the fence and went after him. I heard him scaling the second fence and heard the thump as he dropped down the other side. Swiftly followed by an almighty crash.

Chapter eighty eight

As Dimitri had hit the ground one of the cats had hit him at full speed knocking him back into the fence. By the time I got there both Tyson and Inca were on him. I phoned Vinny and a few minutes later he drove up to me. He put his key-card in the control panel and the gate slid open. 'While I keep them occupied you drag him out. Once you're through the gate, pull my card out of the slot. Go now.'

Vinny was playing roughly with the cats, talking to them in Afrikaans. They obviously knew him well and were happily play-fighting with him. Once I'd got Dimitri through the gate I pulled out the card and the gate began to slide shut. Just as it was about to fully close Vinny dashed through. He checked Dimitri's body.

'Good. They haven't actually eaten any of him. Once a lion does that, it doesn't matter how well trained they are they can never be trusted. They would have to be shot.'

We loaded the body in the back of Vinny's truck. We then drove round and collected the rest. Vinny had radioed Johan and he arrived to help. I dismantled the traps and collected all my kit.

'What's the plan with these then?' I asked Vinny.

Black Heart

'Don't worry I have the perfect place for them. They will not be found.'

I passed him his rifle and night glasses. 'I owe you big time Vinny. I'll see you right tomorrow. And you Johan. Do you think anything will be said about the shot?'

'No. I'ts quite normal for the odd shot out here, especially this close to the park. We often shoot Jackal and other vermin at night. You'll need to move the hire car though. Just park it in the car park at Jack's. We'll go and get rid of these and see you in the bar for a drink in about an hour. The beers are on you by the way!'

We shook hands. 'You bet Vinny, see you in an hour.'

I got in the hire car. The keys were still in the ignition. I drove across the road and up the driveway, parking round the back of Kenjara.

I undid my belt and removed the holster and mag holder. Stuffing them in my back pack I transferred everything to Jan's truck. I went back to the hire car and rubbing my prints from anything I may have touched I locked it and went into the lodge. I had a quick wash and brush up in the gents, and then went through to the bar.

Jeffrey J. Gould

Half way through my third beer I was joined by Vinny and Johan. I downed my beer and ordered 3 more. We sat at a table in the corner. I asked Vinny what he'd done with the bodies. He expained that there was on old, disused well at the back of one of the lion enclosures at the Rhino Park. It was very deep and hundreds of metres from the fence, not that anyone would be likely to go in there! Vinny said he was just glad that Ken was still away and thank God his cats hadn't got the taste for human blood. Vinny'd spent hours with them as they'd grown up and was always entrusted with looking after them whenever Ken was away.

 To their credit neither of them asked who the dead men were. I didn't volunteer the information and the whole subject was dropped. We carried on drinking as if nothing had happened.
As we left the bar Vinny asked me for the key to the hire-car. He said he would drive it out to one of the townships and leave it there with the key in. He'd get a lift back from Johan. The car would not be there in the morning.
As I drove back to the farm I couldn't get that bloody song out of my head.
A wimba-way a wimba-way a wimba-way . . . .

Chapter eighty nine

The following few weeks were pretty uneventful. I got some domestic matters in order.

Jack had shown me how to set up an offshore account.Once sorted he'd transferred my money, minus his commission of course. I bought a nice second-hand twin-cab backie. I took Em to see a few nice properties in the area. We had a few maybies, but I was waiting for Jan to return. We'd decided to make him an offer on his place. Hopefully he'd accept.

If not, then we had a few other options.

I contacted my estate agents back in the UK. Good timing, as I'd had a couple of offers.

I instructed him to accept the better one. It was 15k less than the asking price, but that could be expected, the housing market being as it was. £225, 000. That was, depending on the exchange rates, about 3 million Rand. I could buy a lot of prop' with that kind of dosh.

Before I hung up, the estate agent had said that I had a lot of important looking mail at the house. He asked me what to do with it. I said I'd sort out a forwarding address and ring him back.Jack to the rescue, yet again. When I rang him to ask about opening a post office box he asked me why I wanted one.

When I told him about the mail he'd explained that mail could take weeks to arrive.If it arrived at all. He suggested Jan and Chloe.

They were in the UK for about another week visiting Chloe's parents. He phoned Jan and got the address. I then phoned my estate agents with the address and asked him to courier my mail to them for me.

That had been a few days ago. They would be due back the next morning. As Em and I tidied the house and gathered all our belongings together, I took a break and turned on the TV. I went to CNN. I'd been watching the developments across the pond in the USA.

I turned up the volume and listened to the news 'anchor' man. 'Following this morning's dawn raids by FBI, SWAT and local law enforcement officers, the total amount of arrests stands at 118. We believe further arrests are imminent. All of those arrested face federal conspiracy charges, along with other charges ranging from extortion and tax evasion to 1st degree murder. Unconfirmed reports are linking the arrests to the sudden resignation and withdrawal of the presidential candidate Al Gordon.

We can now go live to the White House, where President Obama is about to address the nation.' The picture switched to the Oval room at the White House and the president began his speech. 'My fellow Americans.Over the last few weeks several of our government agencies, working in conjunction with their British counterparts, for whom we will be eternally grateful, have uncovered a major conspiracy.Upwards of 100 arrests have so far been made in connection with this conspiracy, with more to follow. Presidential nominee Al Gordon has withdrawn his campaign to run for office and, although not arrested at this time, is being interviewed to ascertain his involvement, if any, in this matter.

Upwards of $300m has so far been confiscated, with approximately $200m more expected over the coming few weeks. I intend to see that this money is put to good use where it is needed.Possibly to bolster our welfare system.'

I turned the TV off.Bloody hell. Dinger wasn't kidding when he'd said the shit was going to hit the fan.

Chapter ninety

Jan and Chloe were due back at the farm around midday. We'd already moved all of our belongings back over to Kenjara. I'd insisted that we would pay the going rate for the room this time. God it was all of 28 quid a night! It was a quiet time of the year for Jack and Karen, so it wasn't as if they would be turning away business to cater for us. To me that was an even better reason to be paying.

Em and I had bought and prepared everything to make a full-on breakfast/brunch.

When they pulled up Em got everything on the go. I welcomed them back with a beer and then gave Em a hand in the kitchen. Fifteen minutes later we were all sat beside the pool, tucking into sausage, bacon, eggs, beans, tomatoes etc.

Over our meal we chatted about their trip. We told them how good the dogs had been. Bullshit (actually, the little gits had escaped a few times.)

When Jan went to fetch more beers he returned with my mail from the UK. That would give me something to think about later

We hit them with an offer for their farm. That would give them something to think about too.

Black Heart

We helped clear away the dishes then we made our way over to Kenjara.

Once in our room Em busied herself sorting little Charlie out, so I took my mail out onto the balcony and sorted through it. Most of it was crap, junk mail, the odd utility bill. However, three envelopes got my attention. I sorted them into date order and opened them. The first was from my boss, asking me to get in touch 'as a matter of some urgency.'

The second, also from my boss, ordered me to get in touch immediately, on pain of death.Or worse. By the third, the tone had done a 360. Apparently the 'sun shone out of my arse'and every man and his dog, including Barack Obama, wanted to shake my hand!

Shit. I was supposed to be posing with the president tomorrow. I bit the bullet and rang my boss. To say I got an earful would be an understatement. He was not impressed when I told him where I was. I could hear him ordering people around in the office as he talked to me. The bottom line of the call was that I needed to be at Jo'burg airport by 4pm in order to board a flight that would get me back to LHR. I would then have about an hour to spare, before I, along with him, boarded a flight to Washington DC. Before he hung up he assured me that I was coming out of this 'smelling of roses.'

Oh and I was lucky that I wasn't having 'the book' thrown at me. Then he said, with a hint of pride 'Well done son. Now get your arse back here and make sure you're 'ship-shape and Bristol fashion.'

As I went back into the room I prepared for a second ear-bashing, this time from Em.

She actually took it well, concidering I was packing as we spoke. She'd caught snippets of the conversation with my boss, and when I'd asked her for a pen and paper to write down my flight details, she obviously knew I wouldn't be here for dinner.

Jack, bless him, agreed to drive me to the airport. Em was left to open the bar in case he wasn't back in time. 'Just serve them what they want and write it down. I'll sort it out when I get back. Or Karen will if she gets back first.'

We made good time to Joberg and Jack dropped me at departures with plenty of time to spare.

'Look after the Mrs and sprog for me mate.I'll phone when I know what's happening.I'll try not to forget your 'goodies' this time.'

The 'goodies' in question were the only things Jack missed about the UK.Namely Walkers crisps and Melton Mowbray pork pies. I normally take him some.In my defence I did have a few other things on my mind last time I left the UK!

Black Heart

I shook his hand and grabbing my holdall went into the terminal building.

'Look after the Mrs and sprog.' Yep you're definitely going soft Charlie-boy.

Chapter ninety one

I downed a fair few glasses of red wine on the flight back to the UK. Well it was free, and it also helped me to get some 'shut-eye'. On arrival at Heathrow I didn't have to hang around waiting for luggage as I'd only got hand baggage. I killed time waiting for my onward flight by having a haircut (60 quid!) and buying a designer suit (700 quid!) Not to worry, it's not every day you get to meet the president. Besides, I'd be claiming the money back as expenses!

When my flight was called I went to the check-in desk, where my ticket and visa was waiting for me. So was my boss. We shook hands and his first words to me were.

'You need a shave Charlie.'

'Nice to see you too boss. Don't worry I've got my shaving kit with me. Not much point shaving now. I'll do it just before we land in DC.'

'I take it you've been watching the news? You and your escapades have opened a right little nest of vipers. When we get back from the states you've got a lot of explaining to do before you sign this.' He handed me an envelope. Inside was my letter of

Black Heart

resignation. I was going to resign anyway.Looked like the decision had been made for me.
'Most of the 'Big boys' of organised crime in the states have been arrested thanks to you.
There is one key player that has, so far, not been found. He goes by the name of Dimitri. I don't suppose you know anything of his current location?'
I decided to say nothing for the time being. I just shrugged my shoulders by way of an answer.
We spoke very little on the flight. When I wasn't actually asleep, I pretended to be.
Just before landing I went to the loo to freshen up and shave. Concidering I was nearing the end of a 12500 mile journey I didn't feel too bad.
Once the aircraft had taxied and come to a halt we got a surprise. We were whisked down the steps and into a waiting limo'.
 Half an hour later we were in a swanky reception room at the White House. I sloped off to the restroom and changed into my new 'whistle.' (Whistle and flute-suit)
When I returned we were briefed by one of the presidents aides. He went through the protocol and informed me that I was to receive two medals.The first being The Presidential Citizens Medal, from the office of the President of The United States.

The second, which my boss was also to receive, was the Meritous Civilian Service Medal, awarded by The Defense Intelligence Agency. After the build up, the actual event went like this.In. Shake hands.Given gongs.Shake hands.Photo.Out.

25000miles round trip for that!

If you've never been to Washington DC let me tell you it is basically a museum. Well a conglomeration of them. As we had a car and driver, and several hours to kill before our return flight, we did the tourist bit. I'm not really a museum type of guy, but I had to admit The Smithsonian museum, in particular, was amazing. There were jumbo jets hanging from the ceilings, and a full size Apollo rocket. You could get lost in there. The thing that I found most amazing was the price. They were all free to enter. I thought at first that our 'guide' was flashing some sort of pass or something to get us access. But no, it was free.

If anyone had told me that I'd enjoy wandering around a museum for hours on end I would've laughed in their face.

Yet, here we were, out of time, heading for the airport.

Our driver took us to the VIP Lounge, where we were given the full treatment. Even better, when we boarded I discovered we'd been upgraded to 1st class. Talk about how the other half live.

Black Heart

Back at LHR we were rushed through customs and immigration and out to a waiting car.

Any thoughts I'd had about signing my resignation, leaving it with my boss and legging it had been dashed.

At the office I went through the whole story of Czeckov and Dimitri. Several times. And then a few more times.

I'd been given immunity on whatever I divulged. Well it would look a bit odd if I got arrested for something I'd just received a few 'gongs' for. Even so, I forgot to mention the wife, Davey and Gross!

When the interviewing was finally over I sat in the boss's office and had a glass of single malt with him. He had my signed letter of resignation on the desk in front of him.

'It's been a pleasure working with you Charlie son. I mean that. You look after yourself. I take it you'll be back off to South Africa?'

'Yep, I have a flight booked for tomorrow night. It's been good working for you too boss. If you ever fancy a holiday you know where to find me.' I shook his hand. As I turned to leave I dropped two receipts on the desk in front of him.

'Cheeky twat! Sixty notes for a friggin' haircut and £700 for a bleedin' suit!' I heard him say as I closed the door behind me.

Chapter ninety two

I stood outside smoking a cigarette while I waited for my kebab. It occurred to me that this was the first time I'd had a cig for a few days. (Note to self-pack in bleedin' smoking.)

9.40pm He was bang on time. I stubbed out my fag and went inside. Sitting at the table in the window of the kebab shop, eating my chicken donner with all the trimmings, I watched John Kenny wobble across the road. As he walked into the Lion I got that annoying song in my head again.

A wimbaway a wimbaway . . . .